On the Run
with Mary

Jonathan Barrow

NEW VESSEL PRESS
NEW YORK

ON THE RUN WITH MARY

New Vessel Press

www.newvesselpress.com

Copyright © 2015 The Estate of Jonathan Barrow
First Published in Great Britain as *The Queue* by CB Editions in 2011

Library of Congress Cataloging-in-Publication Data
Barrow, Jonathan
On the Run with Mary / Jonathan Barrow.
p. cm.
ISBN 978-1-939931-24-5
Library of Congress Control Number 2015930105
I. Great Britain — Fiction.

A Note on the Author and the Text

Jonathan Barrow was born in 1947, an hour's drive north of London in Sawbridgeworth, England, the youngest of five brothers. He attended Harrow, the boarding school whose alumni include Winston Churchill and Lord Byron, but never completed his secondary education. Barrow worked at the Dorchester and Claridge's hotels in London before being hired as an advertising copywriter. He published short stories—keenly observed, outrageously inventive parodies of English snobbishness and eccentricities—in *The London Magazine* and exhibited his drawings at London's Redfern Gallery, which has represented leading British artists like Henry Moore and David Hockney. His brother found the closely-typed, much scribbled-upon manuscript of *On the Run with Mary* in Barrow's office drawer the day after the author's death in 1970, at age twenty-two. He died in a car crash alongside his fiancée, two weeks before they were to be married. This book, in which the narrator witnesses and uncannily prophesies what was planned as a wedding turn into a funeral, can be seen as both protracted suicide note and feverish love letter.

ON THE RUN WITH MARY

1

THIS MORNING, SUGAR BUNS FOR three hundred were delivered at the school. As the roundsman drove away, I heard Mr. Prente come up from his basement room. He opened the confectioner's box, counted numbers and found three buns missing. Immediately, he rang the little handbell that he carries in his trouser pocket. Every boy came into the preparation room. Then Mr. Prente searched the lockers. He had difficulty with No. 19 and used a tool. A moment later there was a scream and Mr. Prente ran up the stairs: his gown had blood on it and his underpants were at his ankles. On the way up he bumped against the school hairdresser and oils, clippers, combs, knives and clips fell from the little attaché case which he always carries.

This means the end for the school hairdresser. Only yesterday he had cut off a boy's ear with a clipper and the Head Master now wants to talk to him.

But our Head Master drinks. We know this because he keeps gin in a flap of his gown. Often, we hear him opening tonic bottles during hymns. Often, during a lesson, he would gurp and run to the door. But I would wedge my foot against it and have the pleasure of watching a fully grown man being sick in front of a class of nine-year-olds.

That evening, police came and took away the hairdresser. They have gone to the prison and he will serve his sentence without trial. Mr. Prente leaves tomorrow too. The bursar raided his study and found three hundred pairs of soiled boys' underwear in a chest under his bed. And hidden in a laundry bag, he found 12 lemonade bottles: each overflowing with boys' urine that was still warm. Next morning these bottles were put on display in the assembly hall as a warning to all other members of the staff. Then, after the hymn, each boy filed past and those responsible had to claim their urine. I refused and was thrashed by Mr. Kille before the entire school. (Judging by the wet patch, I guessed that he had an orgasm whilst administering the punishment. Fourteen years later, when we both shared cells at Parkhurst he admitted to me that this was correct.)

Today three more members of the staff left. Mr. Coon, Mr. Peine and Mr. Wese. They took the train to Euston and did not even have enough money for continental breakfast. Mr. Coon leant out of the window in Wood-ford Tunnel and had his head knocked off. Mr. Peine slipped and fell into the WC and died by drowning. And Mr. Wese fell under a taxi on the station concourse and suffered wounds so grievous that he died before reaching St. Bart's.

This tragic news was read out to us at morning assembly. One boy laughed and was immediately summoned onto the platform. The Head Master took an enormous pair of scissors from a leather sheaf and cut the boy in two. This alarmed the entire school, including staff.

Today is his funeral and I have just bought a black tie. The boy's father, an assistant meteorologist from a weather station in the Hebrides, cannot afford his fare home and has to do three days washing up in order to raise the sum. We decide to have a collection for the poor man and I raise 3 pounds 16 shillings and 7 pence from my class alone. But as I was putting this money in a safe place, the Head Master entered. He took away the money and cycled off to the Three Crowns. There he drank heavily and was sick under a laurel as he walked home . . .

I cannot go on like this. Since arriving here as a new boy some 8 years ago, I have learnt practically nothing and seem to spend my life between dramas, police raids, and court-room evidence. Some O-level exams, which once seemed certain, are now rapidly diminishing and I am writing a letter to my father with instructions for my removal from the school.

But the Head Master has a spy-hole into my room and realizes what I am doing. That night, he follows me to the letter box on Goff Common and after I have put my letter in the box, he produces a fish-hook from his waist-coat pocket. He fixes this to a supple bamboo cane and, with incredible precision, hoists my letter into his waiting rucksack. On the way back, he collides with a florist's van but escapes unhurt. The florist, however, receives fatal injuries and dies at the roadside. My Head Master is unaware and pedals on. Then a Mr. Drace appears and kneels beside the florist holding his head until the last moment. The funeral is on Monday and geraniums, violets and snap-dragons from his own shop will decorate the grave.

At 4.30 the next morning I am woken by Mr. Marce, the Head Master's secretary. It is cold in my room but Marce insists that I remain undressed, even though the journey to his superior's study is across several ploughed fields and through two council estates where young children could easily see my dangling genitals. After much pleading, Marce lets me fashion a little loincloth out of an Old School Tie.

Together we quietly leave the house. There is a heavy frost and I feel my urine already freezing in my tubes. So I get out a little paraffin lamp from my rucksack and strap this onto my crotch. This does the trick but several pubic hairs are singed. Mr. Marce, warm in his Shetland sweater, hums my Mother's favourite hymn. As we cross a pasture, I hear pounding feet behind us and realize that we are being chased by a bull. He is cross and snorting. I look at Mr. Marce and notice that terror has made him spend a penny in his pants. Realizing that we can never make it, I turn round and face Bull. This disagreeable animal is astonished and halts immediately. We explain our plight and as tears rolled down my cheeks I noticed that tears were also rolling down Bull's cheeks. Cautiously, fearing a hoax, I approached and put my hand on his neck. Suddenly he went down on his knees, blinked and began to weep. I held his leg and, making a blanket out of Mr. Marce's sweater, covered this sad animal. Between

sobs, he explained to us that the man from the Corned Beef Factory had arrived last night and selected his carcass for the abattoir. For some time, I talked gently to Bull; telling him that it would

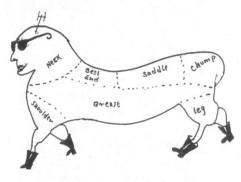

be alright and that we could save him. But suddenly a cock crew on Mr. Stote's smallholding and I saw Bull blink, flinch and roll over. I covered him with straw as best I could and then, with Mr. Marce, walked on.

Now we are in sight of the Head Master's study. This has been specially constructed and is purposeful, set apart from other school buildings. It is a tall, strange building like a lighthouse. A lift has been recently fitted and this takes passengers to the special Thrashing Chamber which is on the top floor. I see the Head Master gazing at us from an upper window. He has my letter in his hands and appears in a poor temper. We arrive at the portcullis and Mr. Marce calls up asking for us to be let in. I hear the Head Master's window opening and a moment later his penis protrudes and he begins to urinate onto me.

I cannot stand it and run away the way I came. But

after a few paces, a noose drops round my neck, tightens and hauls me back. I see the Head Master operating an electric winch and the intense pain is almost unbearable. Slowly, I am hauled upwards towards the little window and, as I reach it, I see the Head Master dart back into his room. I hang there powerless and perplexed for 12 minutes before, mercifully, pain causes me to pass out.

I woke up and saw the Head Master kneeling over me. He appeared excited and I realized that while I had been unconscious my trousers had been tampered with. The Head Master started to stroke me. After that, Mr. Marce left the room for he had to referee an away match that afternoon.

On the way back I stop at a call-box and dial 999. But the desk-sergeant on duty is in a foul mood and tells me to fuck off. In despair I telephone the Chief Constable's private number at Coss Grange. He answered himself and judging from the background noises I would say he was giving a dinner party. When he heard my voice, he put down the phone.

Next day the Head Master tried to take my life. He asked Miss Jogge, the school cook, to place a substance called methlyne oxide in the Roly-Poly pudding, my portion. But before raising the tin spoon to my lips, I detected a curious expression in the Head Master's eyes. My suspicions raised, I gave a spoonful to the mongrel who lives in a basket under the top table. She took it greedily and died four seconds later with a wail so terrible that Mr. Vizze could not be heard to say grace. The Head Master, furious and disappointed, is now chasing me through the school kitchens. Suddenly the tail of his gown catches in a dish-washing machine and, as the propeller revolves, he is dragged into the machinery. He is in considerable discomfort and I switch it off. He begins to cry and I am overcome with remorse. I take him in my arms and, watched by an enormous crowd, carry him gently towards his bedroom. We arrive at his bed and immediately I am overcome by an appalling stench. I pull back the sheets and find that his linen is badly fouled with numerous recent deposits of excreta. Then, to my horror, I find between the sheets the corpse of a boy named H. R. Stort. This 14-year-old had died in the Sanatorium four months ago. Tears stream across my cheeks as I kneel beside him. I did Maths with Stort and knew him well.

At assembly next morning there is a hush as I take my place in the seventh row. An aide walks onto the rostrum and passes a megaphone to the Head Master. He raises it to his lips and calls my name.

Between two aides I am escorted towards the platform. As soon as I step onto the rostrum, the Head Master goes for me with a jack-knife and makes a grievous wound. Then he takes the megaphone again and, with hands shaking, announces to the school that I am to be given the worst punishment ever inflicted on a boy. In fact, he went on to say, he had spent the last four hours consulting International Punishment Records in order to judge the correct severity of the method.

He passes the megaphone to an aide. At a given signal Mr. Cecce, the pianist, plays a loud chord.

I hear a clatter from behind the rostrum curtain and, with another loud chord, the Head Cowman from the school farm appears. With him is an Aberdeen Angus steer. I am taken by aides to a narrow bench. My clothes are removed and placed in a large sanitary bag. I am pushed back onto a bench, manacled and lashed to rings on each side. Then the steer is led onto me and I look up and see the mighty beast's crotch just a few inches away.

Then, to increase tension, the entire school sings Hymn Number 326 Ancient and Modern. I too am forced to sing. Then the Chaplain takes the rostrum and says a few words. Finally the Head Master takes the megaphone again and, so excited he can hardly speak, tells the audience to watch carefully and let this be an example to any boy who dare . . .

Mr. Doode, the Head Cowman, comes over to the steer and gives it an extremely powerful oral enema named Cusci. Immediately I hear rumbles and a torrent of dung cascades onto my face. Unable to breathe, hear or see, I can do nothing save hope that the steer's bowels were not full. They were. Twenty-five minutes later, the torrent still flowed, as powerful as when it began. The Head Master is jumping for joy and is doing a jig with Mr. Marce. But the pupils and masters are silent, horrified by this bestiality. The Head Master, overcome with excitement, can quite clearly be seen to spend a penny in his trousers. And down the hall, I can just see, beyond the blinding waves of excreta, hundreds of my colleagues.

At last the steer's bowels are empty. And with one final, odious fart, he snorts, stamps and is led off the platform by Mr. Doode.

Now pandemonium breaks out. The platform is deep in dung and the masters have to hitch up their trousers. The dung around me starts to harden and the Head Master summons a workman to come at once with a pick-axe. Then I am taken, on a sort of rubber stretcher, to the playground where I am hosed by Miss Akke. After that, she takes me in her arms and, stroking me gently, walks in the direction of my dormitory.

Freeing myself from Miss Akke, I run swiftly through the corridors, dodging masters, boys and a noose that the Head Master constantly slings at me. In moments, I have collected my few possessions and I am dialling for a taxi. Then I run to a laurel at the end of the drive and wait there till the driver arrives. Minutes later I am at the station. The 10.50 is just starting to leave and I do not have time to buy a ticket.

2

FIVE HOURS LATER, AS I STUMBLED ACROSS the Euston concourse with one and threepence on me, dung was still stuck to my thighs.

I queue for an underground ticket. But suddenly, there is a familiar voice behind me. It is Mr. Marce and he tries to slip one of my wrists into a handcuff. I kick him on the shin and he falls clutching himself. Then, hardly able to bear the weight, I carry this man-in-a-mac and slip him into a Left Luggage locker. Sixpence into the slot, the door is shut and all I hear are the very frequent screams for mercy from behind the steel door. He thumps and thunders but no one will hear him. Twenty-four hours later, officials opened the door and he was taken to a mortuary.

Now I must ring my uncle. Once over Sunday tea at Turleigh in 1958, he made me swear that I would ring him if I was ever in a crisis. After queuing for over two hours I found an empty box. But just as I was starting to dial, I saw my Head Master pushing through the crowds and coming my way. A bull-mastiff was at his side and he looked tired and furious. I tried to hide myself but he saw me and, with a squeal of delight, ran to my box. But I held the door and he could not get in. Then, to my horror, I realized that he was trying to topple the box. There was nothing I could do.

It is a strange feeling. The box is on its side and the directories are scattered. I was badly concussed and found a deep wound, from the sharp mouthpiece, on my left thigh. The Head Master's dog is sniffing a few inches away, beyond the plate-glass pane.

I see the Head Master with a small axe in his hand: he is now trying to break the glass and get at me. Luckily, the phone is still working and with great difficulty I manage to telephone my uncle. He is in his bath but promises to be with me in 20 minutes.

The Head Master has now made a small hole in a pane and I see him wheeling a Gas Machine towards me. He switches it on and immediately I smell the dangerous odour. Then he pushes a rubber tubing through the hole, turns up the pressure and watches closely. I feel myself unable to breathe and begin to gasp . . .

I must have been semi-unconscious as my uncle ran onto the platform. The Head Master, unaware of his presence, continued to grunt and smirk as he knelt by the box. My uncle, an ex-commando, fired several shots from his pistol and the Head Master flinched and rolled himself into a ball. Blood flowed from several arteries and his tweeds were all red.

Railway porters kneel beside him and cranes re-erect my box. I see stretcher men running across the concourse.

Then my uncle leaves me, for he has business to attend to. So I am once more left alone on the concourse.

Then I feel something at my feet. I glance down and see a dachshund nosing at my ankles. She is a stray. Together, we walk to the station cafeteria and queue for 25 minutes to get tea and pies. Round her neck is a disc and it tells me that her name is Mary. Born 11.7.53. We find a table in the far corner and I put Mary on my knees. She will not take the pie but is greedy for hot tea that I cool for her in a saucer. Then a manageress appears and tries to take Mary away from me. No dogs allowed in here. Later, she gives in and passes me some wrapped-up scraps, and a collar and lead that a customer had once left.

3

WE GO TO THE UNDERGROUND AND TAKE A TRAIN TO
Charing Cross. There were dense crowds on the platform
and when the doors open I am barely able to board. I hear
the doors about to hiss and close, and tug at Mary. But she
is unable to board for the gap between platform and car
frightens her. With my suitcase I prevent the doors closing and give Mary time to board. The rush hour crowd
gnash their teeth and talk of missed connections.

When we are about ten seconds into the tunnel, a man
next to me starts being sick. He took off his mac and used
it as a receptacle. Ingenious but not foolproof, for large
quantities of it spurted through a gap. I wondered if I
could help. Now he had abandoned the mac and was letting it issue straight onto the duckboards. Other members
of the carriage did not take this too well: for the underground system at this point takes a steep gradient. About
2 in 8. So the pools began to run towards me. Mary was
alarmed and tried to climb up my leg. She is terrified and
her knees are already hidden in the froth. Fortunately,
a nun pushes her way through the crowd and, without
regard for her habit, hugs the man over and over again.

The smell was atrocious and we held the doors open
for as long as possible at Holborn.

I kept an eye on the man and thought he seemed
recovered. But nearing Tottenham Court Road, I saw him
suddenly stand very still. He was starting to go to the
lavatory. He wore a cheap linen suit and the shit pierced
straight through it for the whole carriage to see. Imagine
pressing sauce through a culinary sieve. Just like that. Of
course the stiffer bits were trapped in the inner garments.
Some of the really heavy bits dropped onto the duckboards
and joined the sick as a minor tributary.

Mary was uncomfortable and shut her eyes. She cannot bear unpleasantness.

Then, to the left of me, a woman began having diarrhoea very badly. She was now farting through the diarrhoea (schoolboys do it a lot) which meant that her shit was propelled out like an aerosol. The other, healthier members of the carriage gazed at this miserable spectacle. They wondered if it might ever happen to them.

That night, inspectors from London Transport examined our carriage and decided it was unfit for service. So when the last tube stopped at 00.35 hours, it was shunted, in total secrecy, to the LT Cleansing Sheds at Park Royal. However, the news had broken and press photographers ran along the line. They tried to get pictures—but crafty Permanent Way Engineers had covered the entire carriage with thick woolen fabric.

Far away, in Los Angeles, B. K. Meinheimer III despatched an urgent wire to the LT Board. He urged them to leave the carriage in its original state and pleaded with them not to hose it through.

Meinheimer, an enormously rich man who made a fortune out of a new textile process, now passes his time by running his 'Museum of Foul Curiosities' on Viccuta Blvd., Hollywood, LA. He collects anything to do with vomit and bowels. He is fascinated by such matters as public vomitations and accidental bowel evacuations. He has written over three hundred books on the subject and his *Excreta & Anus Disgraces* is regarded by the universities as the standard work.

He has now arrived at the airport and, hiring a fast limousine, urges the driver to speed to Park Royal. There, perplexed officials are waiting for him. He is shown the carriage and, thrilled and delighted, writes out a cheque for $4,000,000.

After completing the deal, Meinheimer goes straight to the Savoy. But the management shake their head and refuse him entry. Apparently, last time he stayed he drew foul graffarti all over his 7th-floor suite. Technicians employed by the hotel struggled for four months to remove it, but it was indelible.

Meinheimer is livid and finds that he has been blacklisted from every hotel in the postal district. He ends up returning to Park Royal and sleeping in the carriage he has just bought.

He has a troubled night. Pressmen, anxious to obtain photographs, surround the carriage and the constant glare from flash-bulbs makes sleep impossible. At 4.10 a.m. he wants to go to the lavatory. He steps out of the carriage and wanders through the deserted LT executive offices looking for a suitable place to shit. Finally, after searching for an hour, he has no choice but to squat under his own carriage. The pressmen, now numbering at least 40, slip L-shaped lenses onto their cameras and next morning every national daily carries a picture of Meinheimer in a disgusting pose.

Three days later Meinheimer and his carriage depart for New York on the SS Lavatoria.

4

It is a strange, dark evening with yellow skies. Rain falls and the rush-hour crowds begin to run for their stations.

Mary, lost and perplexed, stumbles against every passer-by. Remember that she is an old dachshund. Her sight is dim and her limbs, stiffened by terrible arthritis, cannot bear her weight for long distances. This, combined with her unfortunate circumstances, is too much for her and at the junction of Moorsom Street she sits down and weeps. I take her gently in my arms and walk with her to the Animal Hospital in Ferry Place.

There is a long queue. We sit patiently and an aide brings tea and warm buns. Next to me sits, all alone, a grievously injured rat. He had damaged his foot in a culvert and had walked four miles to find the hospital. Beyond us, I saw moles, hedgehogs, bats, flies, goats, cats, stoats, shrews and dormice . . . Many were in great pain and many passed away before our eyes.

I mask Mary's eyes with a cloth: these are things which a dog of her sensitivity should never see.

Suddenly a most terrible howling from the casualty entrance. I watch closely as a badger, pouring blood, is lifted out of an ambulance. Apparently he had been involved in a collision with an articulated waggon on the A33.

Upstairs, I wander through the operating theatres and see many dumb creatures suffering terrible indignities. In Theatre 6 a donkey is having a limb amputated, and next door I see a mole having his tonsils removed without proper anaesthetic.

In Theatre 9, a hedgehog is having a prostate operation and all his prickles have had to be removed.

That morning, the hospital had received a priority cable from Rhodesia. It warned them that a toad was arriving on Flight 4527 at 10.35 (Heathrow). The toad was dangerously ill and unless treated with the rare serum Ascusi Conci he would almost certainly lose his life.

A general alert was sent to police at Heathrow. A special pass was issued to enable the toad and his handler to avoid customs and baggage check-out. The ambulance drove onto the concrete and, with siren wailing, and 6 police outriders as an escort, journey time to the hospital was just 15 minutes.

Unfortunately he was found to be dead on arrival and his still warm body will be returned to Nairobi on a scheduled 707 tomorrow morning.

After queueing for two hours I at last hear Mary's name called over the Tannoy system. I take her to the surgery and place her on a low padded stool . . .

Suddenly there is a panic in the passage and I hear rushing feet. Three orderlies burst into the room with a tabby-cat. She had taken an overdose and has been rushed to the hospital from her Hyde Park Gardens flat.

The doctor orders a nurse to fetch the stomach pump.

Just then, there is another sound of scurrying feet in the corridor. Without knocking, an orderly runs in with a barn owl in his hands. She had been found with her head in a gas oven and had been rushed to the hospital by taxi.

Mary waits patiently. At last she is again summoned to the padded stool and the doctor, producing a stethoscope, rolls her on one side. He taps her here and there with a rubber hammer and listens carefully to her beating heart. He opens her eyes wide and inspects her teeth. He asks for a small urine sample and passes Mary a flask. But she is unable to produce anything and I have to apologise.

When Mary is out of sight, the doctor asks me her history. I explain that we struck up an acquaintanceship on Euston Station concourse only that morning and that

I understood she was out of work.

The doctor diagnosed neglect and poor nutrition. He gave me a yellow slip which I was to take at once to the all-night chemist at Piccadilly Circus.

On the way out of the hospital, a terrier was rushed past us on a stretcher. He had tried to take his life by leaping off Waterloo Bridge but had been fished out of the Thames by the river police.

5

THE WALK TO PICCADILLY WAS UPHILL AND I STOPPED
constantly for rests. Luckily, in Metton St., a kindly Rolls-
Royce driver stopped and offered me a lift. He lowered
his electric window and asked where I would like to go. I
was about to step in when Mary coughed and showed her
head through a slit in my gaberdine. The driver spotted
her at once and said he detested dogs. I must not travel
with her. He insisted that I should leave Mary in the gut-
ter where she belonged. Then Mary began to cry and the
driver, hearing her sobs and seeing her poor matted coat,
relented and gave her a cushion for the back seat. I was
asked to sit up front alongside him.

After a few minutes I realized that he
was a homosexualist. Though in his 70th
year his trousers were extraordinarily tight
around the crotch and his testicles pro-
truded in an unpleasant fashion. Without
warning, he put his hand on my thigh and
began to stroke. And then he began at my
fly-buttons. I had to look the other way.

Mary was comfortable in the back seat.
She was snoring a little and the tears had
gone.

Suddenly the car began to spin. The homosexualist had devoted too much of his attention to my
pubic areas and had neglected the highway.

Now we were facing oncoming traffic and a collision
seemed inevitable. I saw the front of a truck and the driver letting go of the wheel and covering his face . . .

I was told that the queer died on the way to St.
George's. There, in the mortuary, he was identified as
Marcus Peimenne. They took off his silk clothing and put

them in a dump bin. He had no next-of-kin and lived alone in Stafford Street.

I was pinned under a panel and TD 3728 of the Metropolitan Police knelt beside me. He had taken off his tunic top and this was on my stomach. I tried to feel down but he guided my hand away. In the distance the sirens were wailing louder.

They set up a plasma-drip on the roadside and a crowd gathered.

'Jean, there's a lad dying down there. Don't let the children see.'

I heard the firemen with their cutters and later felt stretcher men wrap me in red blankets.

'Is that lad dead?'

Then they pulled a strap (or girth) around my waist to prevent me rolling during the journey. I saw them wheel a heavy oxygen breather towards me.

Mary could not get up the folding steps and a stretcher bearer, realizing we were acquainted, lifted her. She found the polished flooring tiles in the ambulance slippery and fell several times. Then the stretcher bearer placed her beside me. Immediately she licked at my blood with her rough tongue and found her way beneath the blankets.

But the stretcher man, fearing infection, lifted her away.

Above me the blue flashing light shone through the open ventilation slot, and the siren, deafeningly loud, made my ears hum.

When the morphine began to act, I felt better and began to pick out the well-known landmarks beyond the smoked glass.

But then the ambulance stopped violently. The curved doors were opened and my drivers began collaborating over their A-to-Z. We were hopelessly lost in some sort of cobbled alley. Hens' feathers flew about and there was a stench of fowls' innards. It was a poultry abattoir. There were hundreds of crated dead.

My drivers lifted me down onto the cobbles. And there I lay, under the red blankets, looking up at the evening sky. Mary, tired and ailing herself, was asleep beside me. Then the stretcher men walked away.

Sparrows, chaffinches, crows, rooks, blue-tits, thrushes and larks circled over me. Then a heavy flapping of wings: it was a Golden Eagle staring at me from behind a parapet. He swooped and I felt sick and faint. Luckily, a passing charabanc backfired and distracted him.

My blood had stuck to the stretcher canvas. So, as I got to my feet, skin was torn from my groin and thighs. There were dressings and ointment in the ambulance and I did what I could. They had left the blue light flashing: it was reflecting in windows all down the alley.

I could not find Mary. I searched up and down the alley. Then I heard a noise beyond an open door. It lead into the plucking room of the abattoir. There were 2,000 live broilers ready for tomorrow's slaughter. Mary had got one by the leg. The bird was in agony and there was a deep wound in her breast. She screamed and blood poured from her mouth. Then pandemonium broke out. For in the next hutch there were 500 eighteen-pound turkeys. Furious at Mary's brutality they had broken through their shutters and were white with anger. Hundreds of beaks began to peck at her and it was only my quick reaction which saved her from a terrible death . . .

I took her in my arms and staggered as fast as my injured legs could manage to the main road. I looked back and saw the ambulance and stretcher surrounded by thousands of furious fowls. There were pheasants, partridges, Rhode Island Reds, and, then, with an alarming screech, another consignment of hens broke their hutch and poured out into the alley. Mary, shaking with fear, apologised for her behaviour and promised that it would never happen again.

Suddenly I begin to pee uncontrollably. It must be caused by shock and I am deeply ashamed. In moments, my trousers are drenched and unsightly. I have to wrap my mackintosh tight to hide all trace. Desperate to do more, I run to the GENTLEMEN sign that I see 200 yards ahead.

The attendant will not permit Mary to enter a cubicle with me and insists that she should be left in his booth. I take four rough towels from the pile and run to the end cubicle. In there, I stripped and dried myself. Suddenly there is a knock at the door. Foolishly, I open it and the attendant pushes his way in. He produces his organ and asks if I would like to be dirty with him. Disgusted, I push him away. He leaves at once and a minute later he passed a brief apology note under the door. I acknowledge this at once and I hear him snatch up my note and run to his booth.

I am disturbed from my defecation by a coughing and snuffling in the next cubicle. It is strangely familiar. I go down on my knees and, placing my head as close to the gap as I dare, I try to see who it is. Horrified, I leap to my feet . . . for there, watching me through a spy-hole, is the Head Master. In a desperate panic, I try to get my clothes on—but find that he has cleverly hooked away my trousers and pants. I hear him smirking and grunting and a moment later he tosses a mountaineer's grappling-hook into my cubicle. I crouch in the corner and watch helplessly as he scales the partition. For a moment I think he will lose his balance, but he finds a narrow ledge and hangs from it, kicking at me with his studded brogues. I am at my wit's end and call desperately for the attendant. He comes running and, grasping the situation in seconds, he produces a revolver and fires several shots at the Head Master's wrists. With a horrible scream, he loses his grip and falls headlong into the lavatory bowl. It is still full of my motions and he splutters and begs for mercy. But

I have nothing to say to him and, after dressing, pull the chain. He cannot move for his head is jammed firmly in the bowl, and he suffers appalling indignities. Later I hear that he was rushed to St. Thomas's with asphyxiation and deep wrist wounds.

Once more, I try to make my way to Piccadilly to buy Mary's tablets. She is rapidly sickening and her temperature and pulse-rate alarm me. She stumbles constantly and I carry her for the last mile.

There is a long queue at the prescription counter and there are at least 70 in front of us. Mary, though in great pain, sits calmly on my lap. Next to us sits a drug addict waiting for his next supply. His name is G. L. Husse and his terrible predicament means that he is no longer able to keep his job as a post office counter clerk. He had an experience with Methalin whilst on holiday in Spain and since then has not been able to control his craving. He showed me the dropper-jabs in his arm (like bee-stings) and I sympathised. Next to him there was a young man named C. E. Kenne. He kept his hands over his crotch all the time and I wondered why. Looking closer I realized that he had an erection. Later, I found out that he had been in this awkward position since 3 o'clock yesterday afternoon. He is now waiting for some tablets that will permit the blood to leave his organ—this will allow it to descend.

While we queued, Mary suddenly told me a most appalling piece of news. Speaking in a hoarse whisper, she confessed that she had been a drug addict for 34 years and that she was now suffering withdrawal symptoms from the killer Letharine.

I was speechless and desperate. I grabbed her back thigh and found hundreds and hundreds of needle-marks: blood oozed from many of the punctures and septicaemia was present. I picked her up and hurled her across the room. She dragged herself back to me and, licking at my ankles, begged for kindness, help and understanding. A crowd gathered and a Manager asked me to leave or he would call the police. So I took bruised Mary in my arms and ran out into the street.

6

THE DOORMAN AT THE STRIP-TEASE CLUB SEEMED TO
know Mary and he lets us in for half-price. It was about
2.30 in the morning and the place was full of men. There
was a piano and a low stage. A girl was dancing with no
clothes on and she was doing unprintable things with a
hedgehog and two slugs. We sat right at the back for fear
of being seen.

Mr. Jusse, the manager, brought a bottle of fizzy pop
to our table and a plate of currant buns. Suddenly Mary
jumped off my knee and ran, by way of a ramp, onto
the stage. She stood up on her back legs and showed off
her parts to the audience of 47. They were furious and
booed. Many eggs were thrown and Mary fell to her knees
twice. But undeterred, she continued with her routine. It
was revolting, obscene and indescribable. I blushed and
hung my head. The manager ran onto the stage and tried
to drag her off. But Mary bit him on the wrist and he ran
back to his office with blood streaming down his evening
suit. Unable to find a taxi he had to run to St. George's,
where he was given 19 stitches.

Appalled by these scenes, the doorman dials 999 and
12 minutes later 37 police constables and 3 detective
sergeants made their way down the dark staircase. When
the audience saw them, they rose and ran for the EXIT.
Many got away but several were caught and dragged
upstairs to a waiting police van. When the police saw me,
they ran with truncheons and manacles. I was pinioned
between two constables and taken upstairs. Mary,
completely absorbed by her foul activities, was taken by
surprise. She howled bitterly as a constable flung her into
a blue hessian sack.

The journey to the police station was not without

incident. Our driver had been drinking and was unable to keep the van on the road. We collided with several humans who were killed outright and, at the junction of Pell Street, we ran over a toad that was trying to get from Leicestershire to the South Coast. His legs were badly crushed and his neck was severed. I looked back as we sped away and saw him trying to get on his feet again. Just as he was up, a City Council gutter-cleaning machine came past and swept him into the machinery. After he had gone I found a tiny suitcase near where Toad had been struck down. I opened it, and found 2 pairs of toad's socks, a change of underwear, a cheap toad's plastic mac and a pair of slippers.

As we approached the police station, I saw a constable run out of his shelter and open the heavy oak doors. We drove in and immediately the rear doors were opened and two constables came for us.

We were taken to the cells and locked in No. 8. They tethered Mary's tail and manacled her paws. My clothes were stripped off me and I stood there, miserable and dejected, as the canteen staff came and giggled at my astonishingly small penis. After a few hours a kindly warder named B. K. Ligge came and talked to us. He was a dog lover and, realizing that Mary was of good breeding, brought her the fat from the lamb chop he had just eaten. He said he had a dachshund himself at home.

In the cell next to us, a man was weeping. He is a deaf mute and had stolen a Bible from a Catholic bookshop earlier in the day. He will face Mr. G. Cubbe in court number 4 tomorrow morning.

In the cell on the other side of us, I could make out a man asleep on his mattress. Apparently he had exposed himself in Regent Street. This is his ninth offence and he will probably be sent away. Overcome with sorrow, I stick my hand through to stroke him. But I do not realize that he is only half human: a giant claw shoots out and grasps me. And it is only by the most intense effort that I pull myself free. The wounds to my hand are considerable and I shout for the warder.

Then there is a loud shuffling in the passage. I see 15 men being led into cell 9. There was a strong smell of scents and I saw many silk shirts. They were homosexuals. There had been a raid on an interior decorator's flat in Moss Street. The owner of the house, on seeing the police, jumped out of the window and fell into his greenhouse. His body is at the mortuary now and all London mourns. Obviously the homosexuals have not learnt their lesson. For I can hear huffin and puffin. Masturbation in progress I should think. Then the warden tells them to do up their fly-buttons or forfeit hot tea and muffins. Whichever you prefer.

Throughout the night, there is an awful noise of farting. I call for silence but each time am interrupted by a further bout of flatulence. I trace the source to a Mr. Nomme in cell 19. He is in a pitiful state and is trying desperately to disguise the noise by means of a Pruett's Fart Whistle. This strange device, invented in America by T. L. Ridde, consists of a reed shaped somewhat like a penny-whistle. There is a tuner at one end by which you can adjust the pitch in order to match one's own fart tone. Mr. Nomme carries this with him always (strapped to his waist) and finds it is remarkably successful in disguising his farts. I understand he is toying with the idea of putting it on the market over here. He has approached Harrods— but their Flatulence Contraption Buyer, a Mr. Hinne, is not very interested.

At 8 a.m. I am woken from a troubled sleep by a loud gong. The warder opens the cells and we are lead up to the canteen. Other prisoners from another cell block eye us. We take the end trestle table and food is brought in by women in police blue. Mary politely refuses beans and dripping. But the server takes offence and decides to make an example of her. She takes Mary by the tail and hurls her into a cauldron of boiling porridge. I run to her, but am too late. Her head is now submerging and her bubbles come up through the steaming oatmeal. I dive in my hand but the pain is too much and I withdraw. The server sees me and, with a heavy spoon, strikes me on the neck. I reel back but steady myself on the cauldron handle. Again, I dive in my hand and can just feel Mary's blistered flesh. In tears, I borrow a kitchen scoop and try desperately to raise her. Three police, hearing the noise, rush in and try to pull me away. Then with a mighty effort, I topple the cauldron. Porridge everywhere and Mary staggers from the mess critically burnt.

The court is very crowded and Mary, heavily bandaged, is barely able to climb into the dock. I have to help her and she screams with pain. 25 police cadets, watching proceedings from a long bench, jeer at her and throw paper darts. Several hit her and she snarls at them. The court clock says ten to ten and the Magistrate should have been here long ago. We wait patiently.

A telephone rings in the Clerk of Court's booth. It is the Magistrate, Mr. A. C. Vonne, and he is calling from Little Bickford Station. Apparently he had vomited badly on the 8.34 to London Bridge. He pulled the communication cord and leant out of the window. His linen suit was badly fouled and he caught the next train home. His wife was at the end of the drive with a package containing clean suit, clean shirt, clean socks, clean knickers, clean tie and clean vest. Time is short and he does a quick change on the spot. Mrs. Vonne screens him from pedestrians and traffic with her apron and he does it in two and a half minutes. Unfortunately a police officer passes and arrests him on a gross indecency charge. But after realising the Magistrate's identity, he goes down on his knees to apologise. Mrs.

Vonne takes the fouled garments to the Cleenex Laundry in How St.—but the manageress will not accept them and Mrs. Vonne is obliged to wash them out herself.

We waited for over two hours in that dock. At last I saw Mary prick up her ears and look in the direction of the Magistrate's throne. There was a slamming of doors and the Clerk walked in. He told the court to rise. Then the Magistrate walked in and settled himself on the throne. He was pale and shaking.

Three cases before us. H. L. Kinne found drunk and disorderly in the Strand—staggering along the footrailing. Shouting fuck off fuck off to passers-by. Well, Kinne— what have you got to say for yourself? 10 shillings or 3 days. Time to pay? Certainly not. You've got the money on you.

B. C. Nanne is taken to the dock. Found exposing himself in a public latrine in Pont Street. Nanne earns £6,000 a year as a stockbroker. You must learn to behave yourself in public. Don't let this happen again. £55 or one month. (That night, Nanne threw himself from a window in his Cheyne Row Mansion block. Dead on arrival.) M. L. Quasse is brought in. Found exposing himself in Wyndham's Theatre last night. Stood up in the second act of *Mr. Grant and the Cattle*. Took his prick out and pissed all over the third row of the stalls. A revolting crime. You must go to prison for 16 months.

Just as the next defendant was brought in, I saw the Magistrate go white. He leant to one side and vomited. Immediately the Clerk threw a rug over him and we could not see. But we watched his anguished heaving beneath the wool and felt deeply sorry. With the rug still over him he is taken out of the court by the Clerk. Mrs. Vonne is phoned and takes the next train with a clean change. She comes straight to the court from Liverpool St., stopping en route to buy a tie. She holds him in her arms and comforts him.

The Magistrate is not fit enough to return to court till half past two. So refreshments were brought in by the same woman who had hurled Mary into the porridge. She seemed in a better frame of mind and apologised for her unforgivable behaviour. A sudden depressive fit, she said. We all shook hands.

At last the Magistrate appears. He is hopelessly drunk. The Clerk has to guide him to the throne. His voice is slurred and his breath tells its own story. 7 large gin and tonics. 4 bottles of Medoc. 3 large Leading Ports. 3 Kummels. 5 large cognacs. (This is far too much to drink at lunchtime.)

He is barely able to read the charges. He mistakes Mary for a terrier and this infuriates her. She howls with anger and has to be lashed with the Court Muzzle. Then the Magistrate topples off his chair and, though out of sight behind a wooden pew, can now be heard being most horribly sick.

The Clerk runs for Dettol. A policeman begins to giggle and is instantly dismissed from the force by his superior who happened by chance to be in court. Then there is a long embarrassing silence and all we hear is the pathetic retching from beneath the throne. Mary, now more impatient than ever, growls and yaps. But she is ticked off by Sergeant Winne who kicks her bottom with his boot. She falls flat on her back and has to be resuscitated by the Court Nurse. After more delay and whispering, the Magistrate finally gets back to his throne and proceedings begin.

Stand up when the Magistrate is speaking to you. Mary tried but the bandages were restricting and she fell heavily. A high stool (like you get in bars) was brought and she was obliged to sit on it. Details of our visit to the striptease club and charges were read out and before the Clerk had finished, the Magistrate was standing up and stamping his feet. He was white with rage and hissing. Never in my 49 years as Head Magistrate have I heard of such a despicable charge. It is odious, unspeakable and so vile that I intend to punish you personally. You will return to your cells until I have decided on a suitable punishment.

As we were escorted out, Mary began to weep. Then the Magistrate began to vomit again. As the Clerk ran for the Dettol he skidded on the slime and fell 18 feet down the gaoler's staircase. His neck was broken and a new clerk is on his way from another court.

Back in our cell again. Slops from the night have not been taken away and the stench is appalling. I take off Mary's bandages. The Gaoler is listening to Woman's Hour and I see him taking down a recipe. We wait patiently for three hours. At last we are summoned and escorted, once again, back into court. The smell of vomit still lingers, though attempts have been made to disguise it. There are Airwicks everywhere and an aide is using an aerosol. The Magistrate still looks unwell and has difficulty reading his sentence. You have been found guilty of the most bestial, unpardonable crime. And I intend to deal with you with the vilest severity possible. You will both proceed to the court entrance and a motor-coach will drive you to an area of wasteland some 45 miles from here. I shall accompany you. So shall the Gaoler, the Punisher and 5 Constables.

Mary breaks down and the Court Vet brings smelling salts. She is quaking with fear and tries to plead for mercy. But the Magistrate is in no mood to listen and is already putting on an overcoat. I lift Mary up and wipe away the tears. We walk slowly out of the court between two constables. They try to handcuff Mary but the manacles are too large for her paws. So the Court Blacksmith is summoned from his basement foundry. He brings tools and other devices. He takes off three inches and Mary is held fast. She is fettered around the back paws with rope and, unable to walk, has to be carried into the motor-coach by a constable. I am gagged with elastoplast and fettered with strong rope. A constable carries me and I am placed on the back seat next to Mary.

The Magistrate follows closely behind us. He is still not well and vomits before entering the coach. It goes straight down his tie. The stench is so bad that I have to hold my nose. Mary is asleep already. I can see by the expression on her face that she is dreaming. The guards and constables enter and we are off. The driver takes the A37 and we pass shops and roundabouts for many hours. At 8.30 Mary wakes from a heavy sleep pleading for food and water. But there is nothing and I can only stroke her and try to make her go to sleep again. Several times, the Magistrate comes close and checks that our tethers and handcuffs are still firm. He stinks of sick.

Mary is so revolted that she spits at him. The spittle is slung straight into his eye. He stands up in a most awful rage. He takes Mary by the tail and bashes her against the back of a seat. On and on he goes until she screams for mercy. Blood pours from her and his cuffs are sodden red in moments. The Magistrate, still furious, returns to his seat up front while Mary collapses besides me and falls immediately into a deep and troubled sleep.

It is dusk when at last the motor-coach stops. We are in lonely country and there are no houses. The wind is strong and there are tall trees around us. We are in a glade and are some distance from the main road, having travelled on a rough farm-track for several miles. As we leave the coach the Magistrate whispers to the driver.

We walk over rough ground. Then the party halts. The Magistrate raises a loudhailer to his lips and directs me to a low bench, some 20 yards away. I am made to lie on this and my hands are tethered to a strong ring set deep into the wood. Mary is placed beside me and she is pinned with ropes and hooks. I can't think what is about to happen. The Magistrate yells something into a loudhailer and immediately, through the dusk, I see a cowman approaching with a bullock. The animal is brought to us and made to stand directly above our bench – with his legs on either side of us. I glance up and see the crotch just a few inches away.

The Magistrate speaks to the assembly. Then they sing a hymn. The cowman comes to the bullock and with a hypodermic, injects a vein with a powerful anal emetic called Cusci Russa. A moment later the rumbles start. I try to cover my face. But my hands are tethered. There is nothing I can do. Mary lies on one side, trying desperately to shield herself. The first odious torrent cascades over us. Unable to breathe, hear or see, I pray that the bullock's bowels are not full. But they were. For 25 minutes later the torrent of excreta still flowed. The Magistrate, thrilled at the success of his novel punishment, is leaping about and urging the bullock to continue his motion as long as is possible . . .

Then a strange thing happens. The bullock suddenly turns his head and whispers to Mary. Of course I do not understand what they are saying but, gathering from Bullock's expression, I would guess that he was desperately sorry for what he had done. Mary then turned to me and translated. Bullock says he is embarrassed and distressed. He is asking if there is anything he can do to make it up. Mary says yes. Will you please be so kind as to butt the Magistrate with your horns. Bullock agrees willingly, and, when the Magistrate's back is turned, he charges at him. The horns penetrate the arse and blood appears. The Magistrate lets out a scream and spins round. Bullock charges again and again. Magistrate crumples and falls. He lies in a tractor rut suffering critical abdominal injuries. But Bullock shows no mercy. He walks up, gets astride, and excretes directly onto the Magistrate's face. He is smothered in seconds. The guard runs to his side. But he is hardly able to breathe. His pulse is weakening and the heart irregular. One constable tries the kiss of life but is prevented because the throat is choked with bullock excreta. There are deep wounds centred round the lemeal artery. There is nothing more to do. Forty-five seconds later he passes away and, as his eyes close, he lets out a little cry.

A priest comes running from a nearby farm. He does the last rites. Then a storm begins. The skies open. Lightning and thunder. You can just see the ambulance making its way down the rutted farm track. But the rain is so dense that they have difficulty. Rigor mortis has set in and the Magistrate is hard to move. The stretcher men use crowbars, winches and pulleys. It takes over an hour. I tip them 10 shillings each.

Mary is drenched and shelters inside my coat. She is not well and I handle her carefully. I must get medical aid. The bullock asks which way we are going. He offers us a lift on his back as far as the main road. I help Mary up and jump on. Bullock walks slowly, careful to avoid potholes and sharp stones. He leaves us on the broad grass verge at the point where the B48 meets the Great North Road. As he plods away, I shout a final message of farewell. But he is deep in private thought and does not hear.

7

WE ARE OVER 200 MILES FROM LONDON. THE DISTANCE depresses us and we decide to lie in the long grass till dawn. I lay out my coat; Mary gets onto it, lays down her head and falls asleep at once. I try to sleep but the exhaust and noise from the overnight road-freighters disturb me. So I lie there aching and exhausted, the bitter taste of excreta still in my mouth.

At 4.38 a.m., just as the sun is coming up over Gorley Woods, I hear a strange rustling in the grass beside me. I peer closely but can see nothing. But there it is again. Suddenly I leap to my feet and go pale. For there, just a few feet away, is a 19-foot Viper. It is curling itself into a ball, ready to strike. He is as thick as a man's neck. I see his eyes—like green pins. They are staring at me. Then he begins to hum. Mary still sleeps on, unaware of the danger she is in. I snatch the coat from under her and hurl it over Snake's head. He lets out a furious cry and bites angrily at the mackintosh fabric. Little bits of venom penetrate the waterproof and are visible from my side. Like eye-drops. I snatch Mary in my arms and run as fast as I can. The snake throws off the mac and chases after us. He is determined to overtake us and he pants and screams. I run into the Great North Road. I see a Shell oil tanker making for me. I dive for the centre island. Mary screams. I see the driver, his face screwed up, desperately trying to control the skidding vehicle. With a final mighty effort I throw myself clear. I land on the grass island with one shoe still on the asphalt and a long tear in my coat. There is a terrible cry from behind. I glance over and see that the rear wheel has gone over Snake. He is trapped and in agony. I run to the driver who is too shaken to talk. I take the pistol from under his seat and put an end to the misery. One shot does it. The snake's skull bursts and I see the most frightful things. Mary covers her eyes. She hates death. The driver gets down from his seat. He can hardly stand; I steady him and pour strong tea from his billy. A line of traffic has built up behind. I see police with blue flashing lamps and sirens pushing through. An ambulance man throws a rug over Snake. They do not want to take him in the ambulance. So a workman, on his way to Goston pottery, takes the body and throws it far into the bushes.

It is five past five. After walking for some distance down the Great North Road, I see lights from an all-night transport café. Heavy lorries, trucks, carriers and artesian vehicles are parked outside. I long for strong tea and a grill. The drivers, six to a table, begin to jeer when they see Mary. They hurl scraps at her. She is hit in the eye by a grilled kidney. I complain at once to the proprietor. But he takes violent offence and grasps Mary by a leg. Then, as other drivers crowd round, he dangles her above his 180°F deep-fat fryer. She screams and snaps at him. He lowers the tip of her tail into the deep-fat fryer. Mary bears the intense pain bravely but I can see from her glazed eyes that she is in agony.

An animal-lover pushes his way through the crowd. He tears Mary away from the proprietor and, after stroking and calming her, passes her gently back to me. Her tail is terribly burnt. She must not be allowed to see: I mask her eyes. The kind driver, determined on revenge, grasps the proprietor and tips him head-first into the deep-fat fryer. Immediately there is a smell of burning flesh. The stretcher men have to wait three hours for the fat to cool before corpse removal. I try not to look.

Again, we set off down the Great North Road. I try to hitch a lift but each time the driver scowls. At last, a milk truck driver slows down, glances and stops. I step up into his cab. But the driver, when he sees Mary, pushes me away.

We walk on for eight miles. The vehicles sling up dense black mud. We are sodden and filthy. I long for hot water and a bath. (A police patrol stops at ten to six to see if we are vagabonds or men of the road.)

As we turn a sharp corner, I see a milk lorry on its side. There has been a collision. Firemen with cutters try to release the driver, trapped by his own chassis. A surgeon from the Royal Institute passes with a wife and three children en route for Inverness. He offers help and fears double amputation. They have difficulty with the hypodermics because he is tense and shaking. So he swallows morphia pills. The churns are all over the asphalt and milk, six inches deep, covers the road. Already, thieving catering officers from local prisons, asylums, institutions, mad-houses and rest-homes are there. They bring stirrup pumps and other apparatus. Mary, her throat dry and parched, laps at the milk. She is seen by a constable and truncheoned on the neck. She collapses into the milk and takes a lot in. She chokes, splutters and goes blue. My hands dart to get her. I take her on the verge and apply Kiss of Life. Unfortunately, a police officer is watching us. He thinks I am buggering her and walks over to intercept. I explain that there has been a mistake. The police vet is summoned: he takes Mary to his mobile surgery and examines her private parts for tell-tale evidence. But he finds nothing and the charge is dropped. The constable apologises and offers us tea from a police flask.

We set off once again. After half-an-hour, a black Cadillac pulls up. The electric side window is opened and I hear Beethoven's 5th Symphony on the stereo (an eerie sound at that hour). I peer in. Immediately my wrist is grasped by a feathered claw. Petrified, I pull back. I try harder but my captor is stronger. Now we are face to face. It is a giant wood pigeon – at least the size of a fully grown man. The claw lowers and tries to fumble with my fly-buttons. I punch at it. But it now has my penis firmly in the claw. Mary comes to the rescue. She takes a deep bite into Wood Pigeon's neck. With a frightful cry, he falls back, slumped across his steering wheel. Mary and I collapse on the curbside. Wood Pigeon just manages to get the car into first and, with a huge roar, it tears away. But it is hopelessly out of control. Wood Pigeon, blood pouring from the wound, tries desperately to keep control. Now the car is in the wrong lane and a collision with a Morris Estate follows immediately. Wood Pigeon is flung through the windscreen and spins three hundred yards, ending in a tall elm. I should imagine he would have lost his life.

No car stops. We have no alternative but to walk on. After a few miles a hedgehog comes out of the undergrowth and holds up his hand signalling us to stop. I put Mary down and she goes up to talk. He asks if she could get him to the other side of the road. He has been trying for two weeks, but each time had been driven back by traffic. At this point there are 6 lanes and, at peak hours, it would be a treacherous journey. Mary willingly agrees. She kneels down and Hedgehog climbs on her back. I take off my tie and strap it round Mary's neck (so HH will have something to cling to). They set off. Mary goes carefully and, with unaccountable skill, dodges even the fast vehicles. On the centre reservation I watch them take a rest. Then they are off again. After that I lose sight. I wait anxiously for 7 minutes and am relieved when Mary appears. She is not in a very good mood. The hedgehog hadn't thanked her. He just ran off into the bushes.

We walk on. I wave at every car, lorry and van. But none stop. But after another mile or so, a red Consul stops. The driver, a friendly dress-shop assistant, tells us to jump in. He will gladly take us to Bennet Crossroads, a good 50 miles south. We are both thrilled and Mary licks his wrist. Just as we open the rear door, I notice a familiar figure hunched in a corner seat. I have no difficulty in recognizing my former Head Master. He sees me at once and immediately aims a kick at my private parts. He scores a direct hit on the right testicle and, in unbearable pain, I fall straight into his lap. I struggle and kick at him. Mary begins to bark and dance about. She bites at his ear and takes off the lobe. This just makes him angrier and he grabs my penis and stretches it up like an elastic band.

I scream with pain and punch his crotch. Then, with incredible speed, he removes his trousers and tries to get into my back passage. This is the final insult and with the help of a pair of dress-maker's scissors kindly lent by the driver I snip at his penis. He manages to dodge, but, all the same I take a sizeable chunk from the scrotum and he is now out of action. He lies sobbing on the floor, and after returning (and disinfecting) the scissors to the driver I leave the car.

8

I CANNOT GO ON LIKE THIS. I HAVE BEEN WALKING FOR three hours and have got nowhere. Suddenly I see a sign saying TO THE STATION.

Mary, thrilled at the thought of warm carriages, runs ahead of me. We climb steep stone steps and, dodging the ticket office, hide ourselves away in the waiting-room. There are no other passengers about. I check a timetable and find that the next train to London is in just over an hour. I wander about. The station cafeteria is closed. I ask a guard why. He says the manageress is badly hung-over and will not be on duty today. But he gives me the key and says I can help myself. This is good news. I call Mary. I call again. I hear her somewhere. After searching deserted waiting-rooms, offices and other parlours, I find her in the luggage office. She is barking at a wicker crate. She appears to be excited. I look closer at the crate and find, to my horror, that it was supposed to have been des-patched some 7 months ago. Inside, lying on their backs, are two dozen dead bantams. The stench is terrible and I try to get Mary away. I ask a guard what has happened. He says he is not interested and threatens to throw me under a passing train if I persevere with my enquiries.

There is a thunderous noise in the distance. Then, with whistle blowing, a nonstop Perth–London hurtles through. I glance at the carriages. To my utter astonishment I see that the faces that peer from the windows are not those of humans. There are gorillas, giant bats and orangutans. Many appear dead, for the skin is pale and stretched. I query with the guard. He threatens to throttle me if I still persist. Another strange noise comes from the direction of the cutting. A single goods truck appears, propelled by the gradient. I gaze at it, fascinated. For inside, heaped one upon the other, are at least 200 dead rats. Their whiskers twitch in the wind and their eyes still water. In moments the truck has passed and I go at once to the guard and enquire. He produces a pistol and threatens to shoot me if I cannot learn to be less inquisitive about matters which do not concern me.

There is still half an hour to wait for the London train and, anxious to avoid any more peculiarities, I urge Mary to come with me to the cafeteria. When we get inside, we are both struck by a strong smell. I open the roasting ovens and am horrified to find that, in one of them, there is a strange joint of meat set at Ratio 4. I take it out and place the joint on a marble slab. It appears to be the texture of veal and is neatly trussed with string and two pine skewers. But somehow the smell is too acrid and pungent. Then to my horror I realize I am looking at the remains of a man's hand. Feeling sick and faint I run out onto the platform and throw this foul joint down onto the lines. In a few moments, I see the guard hoist up the hand by means of a long hook: he returns to his office, and after flavouring with salt, pepper, mustard and horseradish, he proceeds to eat the hand. I notice him spitting out some of the tougher sinews. Later, he vomits into his little bowl.

There is still 20 minutes to wait, so I cross by the subway to Platform 2 where I can see a newsagent's kiosk. However, just as I walk up, the assistant drops the little green shutter. I knock, but he will not open up. There is chattering and laughter. I knock again. Immediately, the shutter opens and I witness an extraordinary sight. The assistant has taken all his clothes off and has obviously been abusing himself. His penis, measuring over 11 inches, is erect and his face is flushed. He is also breathing heavily. Then, with a deft movement, he places his stiff penis just beneath the shutter. He holds it there and, leaning back, drops the shutter directly onto his organ. This is split in two instantly by the sharp little ridges that are set into the base of the shutter. The assistant lets out a shameful cry; I run round to the back door to assist and comfort him. But the door is locked and he will not let me in.

Disturbed by these incidents, I return to my bench on Platform 1. After a few moments, I hear the station announcer system being switched on. There is loud crackling, then heavy breathing. Obviously the microphone is in amateur hands. Then a revolting thing happens. The announcer holds the microphone to his anus and amplifies a long spluttering fart. It continues for 38 seconds and I wonder if it will ever stop. As soon as it ceases the announcer does a tittering laugh and tells a very rude joke. I cannot bear it any longer and am determined to put a stop to this lunacy. However, as I get to my feet, the announcer takes the microphone and even more filthy noises are amplified. I hear the sound of a man vomiting. A horrible, foul sound that is totally unnecessary and an insult to both myself and Mary. I take a brick and throw it at the amplifier that is fixed high up in the roof supports. Immediately there is another long burst of farting, followed by gurps, hiccups, oathes, curses and further vomit effects. (I cannot stand it and bury my face in my hands.)

In the distance I hear the sound of the train. Then Mary suddenly tugs my cuffs. She has noticed that the guard is behaving suspiciously. He is down by the points lever and he has pulled it over. I run as fast as I possibly can. For I realize immediately what the villain has done.

 He has now diverted the express onto an old branch line. The track runs for just a few hundred yards and after that it peters out. If the express takes this line, it will mean certain death for every passenger and possibly the worst rail accident in history. The guard sees and runs for me. But I am too quick and, just in time, pull back the lever. The guard, white with rage, produces

a Luger and aims for my heart. Mary, with superb timing, jumps at him and tears a wound in his neck. He falls to the ground with blood gushing from a severed jugular artery (Mary stops to lap some up—but I hurry her on). The train driver, unaware of his escape from peril, scowls at us for being on the track. We step on board, thankful to be leaving. As the train pulls out, I look from my window and see the guard doubled up by the track in excruciating pain. Finally, realising that a slow death is inevitable, he takes his own life by tilting himself into the pounding wheels. (Nobody saw this except me.)

9

I walk the length of the train. It is over-loaded. Twelve passengers to a compartment and more line the corridors. As I push past they stare and try to trip me. With Mary under my arm, I go to the restaurant car. But the steward will not admit us. He covers the doorway with a table cloth. So I peep through a gap and see a most horrifying sight. Cooks, galley-hands and waiters are crowded round a table. Feathers are scattered everywhere and I see a hen lying on its side. They are torturing it with red-hot wire and pincers. I beg them to stop. Then Hen rises on her haunches, wails and falls back again. She has passed away. The stewards take the body and toss it out of the dining-car window.

I watch the carcass skid down an embankment and roll onto the A4. A motorist, thinking it to be a human limb, pulls up and places it in his boot. He drives away. After a few miles, he hears clucking and, through his rear mirror, sees the hen getting out of the boot. Her heart had begun to beat again and, with a supreme effort, she had managed to open the boot from the inside. The driver is so astonished that he loses concentration and swerves into the wrong lane. He is hit by a laundry van and flung through the windscreen. He dies in the ambulance. But the hen, with amazing agility, jumps just before impact and manages to fly to a nearby poultry farm. She goes to the farm-house, knocks on the door, and is received by Mr. Mille. He is delighted to accept her services and offers tea and biscuits. That night, while the other 23,000 Rhode Islands are roosting he shows her to her hutch. Next morning, the other fowls take an instant dislike to the newcomer. They set on her and the angry farmer is obliged to keep Hen in his own house. For two years she was the ideal

hen and the farmer grew passionately fond of her. Unfortunately a local gossip called Miss Cudde started a story that the farmer was having an affair with Hen. This came to the ears of the CID and one night, though believing the story highly improbable, they felt obliged to make a raid. It was at ten minutes past midnight. Three police cars, Alsatians and a black maria arrive at the farmhouse. The farmer, clad only in a jock-strap, refused them entry. But they waved a search warrant and he was forced to admit them. They ran upstairs and found Hen lying in his bed. She was naked and in a state of high sexual excitement. The inspector, sickened by such a revolting crime, immediately arrested both hen and farmer. A month later, Judge Matthew Licce sentenced the farmer to 28 years hard labour for this bestial and hideous crime. (He broke down and was dragged to the prison bus.) Then Hen was brought into court in a crate. The proceedings were complicated by the translator who had difficulty in getting the hen to speak up. After considering the evidence carefully, the judge advised the jury to return a sentence of not guilty. Hen, thrilled by her free pardon, ran out into the town and got most frightfully drunk at the Dog and Duck. After closing time, the landlord threw her out and she wandered about the town in a very pissed-up state. She found a bench to sleep on by the bus station. Unfortunately she was set on by a gang of youths. They raped her and kicked her face in. She was so upset that she went to the bus station toilet, jumped into the bowl and flushed herself away to die a terrible death by drowning in some dark sewer.

I continue my journey down the length of the train. There must be a seat. The inspector is surly and suggests I stand like the others. Exhausted, I search for a vacant WC where at least I could sit. But all are engaged. Long queues have formed outside each one. Many cannot wait and are openly pissing. I see smoke pouring from under a lavatory door. Disturbed, I knock and rattle. I hear a moaning noise and the smoke pours even thicker. Now I am really worried. With the help of a wrestler returning to London after appearing the night before at Manchester Town Hall, I manage to break down the door. A horrifying sight awaits us. A man has set fire to himself. I scoop into the lavatory bowl and douse the flames. He lies on the floor shuddering and groaning.

At last we find a compartment with a few seats spare. I fall asleep at once, tired by the ceaseless commotion that now forms such a major part of my life. However after half an hour, I awoke suddenly. There was a man's finger on my fly-buttons. I brushed it away.

As the train nears Buckingham, an old lady dies in Compartment 8. I see her drop and run to bag her seat. Others follow me; there is a scuffle but, with slight force, I manage to claim it. Inspectors appear and take the deceased to the goods compartment where they will go over her. She was a Lady Ruffas and her woman's magazine, half-read, still lies by her seat. (The coat, handbag and purse have already been stolen.) The other passengers have already forgotten the incident: they gaze at the fields, sleep or work at crosswords. I settle in my newly found seat and with Mary stretched across my lap am soon lulled to sleep by the heavy pounding of the wheels. I wake violently. Once again, someone has their fingers on my fly-buttons. A voice, realizing that he has been discovered, pleads that he may be allowed to continue. I jump to my feet, kick the interferer in the private parts and pull the communication cord. I brace myself for the sudden braking—but, instead of stopping, the train seems to go faster. I pull again. And again. In a furious temper, I rush from the compartment and make my way to the driver's cab.

An inspector tries to stop me entering. He says the driver must not be disturbed. He must keep his eyes on the lines and signals ahead. Throwing him aside, I rush into the cab and am horrified to see that the train is not being driven by a human being. For, crouching at the controls, is a giant rat at least twice the size of a man. Sweat pours from his face and he is obviously in difficulties. We are going far too fast. Thankfully, I find the automatic control lever and immediately the exhausted rat falls back into my arms. He pants and sobs and urges me to throw him out of the window. I refuse. I ask him if he would like to talk it over. He shakes his head and, with a final farewell, leaps onto the ledge. He gets the window open and jumps. There is a frightful scream, and I stagger out of the cab. Sadly, I return to my compartment.

En route for my compartment, I notice that smoke is pouring from underneath a locked lavatory door. Perturbed, I rattle and knock, but cannot gain admittance. Soon the whole carriage are opening their sliding doors and looking out into the corridor. The door is flimsy and, with several kicks, I bash it down. Beyond is a familiar sight. A man has tried to set fire to himself with kerosene. He is lying face-up on the floor. I ask if there is a doctor on the train. A short, bald man pushes his way through. He says he was struck off 12 years ago but will do all he can.

Mary is missing from my compartment. I ask my fellow passengers but they know nothing. Positive that they are hiding information, I produce a thumbscrew from my pocket and hold it above my head for the whole compartment to see. Immediately there is a chorus of suggestions. She went this way. She went that way. She went to the toilet. She was bored. She lost her way . . .

After much searching I at last find her in the goods van. She is weeping. I notice three sides of smoked salmon hanging just above her. It is a sad story. Apparently as she was passing the goods van, she heard one of the salmon crying for help. It was not properly dead – for Lord Unce, who caught her in the Spey last week, had hooked her badly. Mary, kind and sympathetic as always, held her hand and promised she would do all she could to ease the misery. The worst part is that the three sides had all been great friends since school. They had shared flats together in London and were all planning to visit the World Fair next Autumn. The salmon says that the worst part of the ordeal was when they were put in the smoke-hole in Inverness. It was like someone puffing cigarette smoke at you. And the awful thing was watching her friends go from bright pink to ochre. The memories brought tears to her eyes. Suddenly she let out a most terrible scream, lifted herself from the hook and threw herself onto the floor. Horrified, we gazed down. The neck was broken in two places and blood streamed from arteries. Four minutes later, she was dead. I wrapped her in a napkin and, as the train passed over the River Avon, I threw her out of the window. It was an appropriate burial.

We return to our seats. On the way, I see a compartment with the blinds down. Curious, I peep through a gap and watch two homosexuals behaving illegally. They do not know that I am watching. Stupidly, I sneeze loudly. They hear, see and cover their parts with handkerchiefs. They are very angry and chase me down the corridor. I hide in a toilet but cannot get the Engaged sign to work. So they push in and, pinning me against the wall, attempt many unprintable things. My clothes are ripped and taken off me. One homosexual takes a pair of scissors and, with deft snips, trims away all my pubic hairs. Then I was forced to watch one of them going to the lavatory. Afterwards, stark naked, I rushed back down the corridor and hid in what seemed the nearest compartment. Inside are four debutantes all aged 17. They are writing invitations for their May dance in Worcestershire. They had never seen a naked man before and hid their faces. However, after talking quietly to them, their embarrassment vanished. In turn, they examined my parts and had immense satisfaction in seeing a stand. They offered to show me their bits but suddenly feeling out of place I refused. Suddenly there was a loud knocking at the door. It was one of the girls' mothers. She was livid and white with rage. She ran for the guard. You must never see my daughter again. How dare you. Where are your clothes. Who are you. Get out. How dare you.

I covered my parts as best I could and was thrilled, just as I left, to be handed a slip of paper by one girl. It was an invitation to meet her in the first-class lavatory in 20 minutes' time. I began to shake with fear. You see, I have never taken a woman and doubt my powers. I found a quiet corner with Mary and begged her to tell me her own sexual experiences. When she was 16, she went to a cocktail party and met a bulldog called David. That night, after a long drunken dinner in Ristorante Quixinto Inmexo, he fucked her. I poured

out questions about the actual experience, but she grew shy and whined. Since that night, over 46 years ago, she told me she had had a great many dogs and several cats too. And once in Dublin, a frog.

Reassured, I begin to look forward to the pleasures that lie ahead. I think back to all the sex books I have read and rack my brains to recollect diagrams, maps, keys and other directions. Luckily I found a copy of *Gray's Sex for the Young Man* tucked into my inside pocket. There are helpful hints and anatomical drawings. So, with just 10 minutes to go, I rapidly examine the relevant chapters and carefully study the diagram on page 18. This is interesting. Someone has added hand-drawn organs. My pulse quickens and tell-tale eruptions appear at my fly-buttons. Ashamed, I place the daily paper on my lap; but the power beneath is too strong and the paper is toppled off. Suddenly the sliding door is flung open and the Girl's Mother enters. She seizes the book and, shaking with rage, clutches me by the neck. With extraordinary power she rips off my makeshift trousers, snatches my stiff penis and circles it with strong bailing twine. Then with a triumphant smile she departs. The pain is excruciating and I urge Mary to bite through. She gnaws furiously and after another 8 minutes of agony I am free again. My angry penis, outraged by this attack, hurls unprintable abuse.

I rush to the meeting place. Just as I am entering, strong hands grasp my waist. It is the Girl's Mother again and she has with her a pair of giant hedge-clippers. I guess her intentions, snatch the clippers and throw them through an open window.

Unfortunately, they fall onto a main road, and a gas-fitter, cycling to Woodley, was struck by the open blades. His wrist was severed and he fell from his machine. I feel frightful about it.

Girl's Mother, realizing the game was up, returns to her compartment. Again I enter the lavatory. In there, wearing only knickers, was the girl. We shake hands and I place the sex book, open at the correct page, on a ledge. I stand beside her, place my hands on her garment and lower. I am astonished. She has the Private Parts of a man. I am bitterly disappointed and am just about to leave when I notice a small object on the floor. It is covered by a cotton handkerchief and is roughly the size of a sausage. It is a man's penis. The girl blushes. I grab her arm and beat her about the face. After further torture, she admits that her 'penis' is a polythene 'screw-on' bought last week at a Holborn joke shop. I run from the room in total confusion.

A man in a corduroy suit, red socks and dishevelled hair is leaning out of a window. He looks wretched. His eyes are red with weeping. There has been a tragic incident. Last Tuesday he had finished his 90,000-word novel which had taken 9 years to write. He was now on his way to London to present the manuscript to Gilda & Godwin, Gilston St. publishers. But as he was passing an open window, a strong gust blew every sheet out of his hands. He was left clutching an empty file. I held his hand and comforted him. But, overcome with sorrow, he lowered the sill, and threw himself out. I got a turn-up but, because the material was cheap, I was left with just a handful of corduroy. Far below on Exton High St., I saw a crowd of shoppers gather round the body. That night, the editor at Gilda & Godwin was told the news. A man of action, he cabled Exton Technical College and asked them to send out volunteers to search tracks, sidings and cuttings to gather the lost work. With great diligence, the task was successfully completed and four days later all 14,000 sheets were despatched to London. Despite sodden and almost illegible pages, the book was published on April 11th. It was an immediate success and the young writer was acclaimed, posthumously, as a genius. His body was exhumed from the Salvation Army graveyard, where he had been given a pauper's funeral, and taken to London for a memorial service at Westminster Abbey. Unfortunately the hearse collided with a No. 5 bus in Parliament Square. The coffin, split in two, fell open in front of a crowd of gasping celebrities. Screens and capes were rushed to the scene. No press photographers allowed.

10

THE TICKET-COLLECTOR APPROACHES ME. HE WANTS TO know the whereabouts of my ticket. Then he asked if Mary had a dog ticket. Then he insulted us. You are a disgrace to the train. You must leave us at the next station. I have arranged for you to be collected and taken to a Home for Imbeciles.

I push him away and run to a secret hiding-place in the goods van. Twenty minutes later, I hear the train suddenly pulling up. I look out. We are at the tiny Rollscliffe Halt with two stopping-trains a day. It serves a hamlet of 23 people. There is a public house and a sub post-office.

The inspector runs along the platform. It is bright and sunny. He has a megaphone in his hand. Come out now. Otherwise we shall come in and get you. I shake with fear. Unfortunately, Mary farts and an alert passenger hears and detects. We are dragged from our hiding-place and taken onto the platform. Heads stick out all down the train. Rotten fruit, vegetables, dead cats, bad eggs, sewerage and chemicals are slung at us by the furious passengers. The imbecile asylum attendants, anxious to put me under their care, run onto the platform and bundle me into a canvas sack. It is a thick material; I cannot see through it and breathing is difficult. There is so little room. I am doubled up and my head is ducked. Mary, upside-down, crouches on the bottom. I hear them lashing the top with wire. Then I hear the train leave.

It is very quiet. I hear larks, thrushes and, in the distance, a tractor ploughing. Strong hands take the sack; it is taken down the station steps and placed on the waiting imbecile truck. They have difficulty heaving it and three passers-by are summoned to assist.

A handler jumps on the waggon and whispers into my

sack: You are now going to a Home for Imbeciles. It is a lonely asylum on a moor, some twenty miles from here. You will be taken care of. Everything possible will be done to ensure your comfort.

We set off. At Ancaster, the truck stops and three more canvas bags are loaded. Each contains an imbecile. They do not appear to be proper humans and no conversation takes place. One imbecile tries to escape by throwing himself off at a traffic light. The driver notices in his rear mirror and the imbecile is held back. As a punishment, he is taken out of his sack and placed on the road. His feet are tied and connected by a long strong rope to the rear bumper. We set off again and the screams from the foolish imbecile are painful to hear. After another 10 miles the truck stops and he is put back into the sack. Half his back and thighs have been rubbed off. A terrible sight.

It is a painful and arduous journey. As we go over Carter Bridge, a truck draws alongside us. I hear grappling hooks being slung over. Someone is trying to get me. Beyond the canvas, I can just make out a familiar figure. It is my Head Master. He is throwing the grapplings and swearing every time he misses. He is urging me to give myself up. Suddenly I feel something lodging itself in the canvas above me. A hook penetrates, grips and I am pulled into the air. My lorry stops. The handlers have noticed. They run out and urge the Head Master not to make a nuisance of himself. Otherwise we will have to call a policeman. He jumps onto the cab roof, takes down his trousers and pisses onto them. This is politely ignored; the handlers have had many years of asylum experience and see it every day. They call up and urge him not to behave ridiculously. But excited by the experience, he squats and starts to shit. Unfortunately, during the evacuation, he loses his balance and falls 16 feet onto the asphalt.

The truck is too wide for the lodge-gates at the end of the asylum drive. It jams between the granite pillars. Pneumatic drills and explosives are summoned. But we are stuck fast and transferred to a handcart. The drive is long, steep and winds through privets, laurels, antirrhinums and rhododendrons. I see inmates resting on benches, and tethered to the verge are strange half-humans, half-animals. They hum tunes to welcome us. Our carriers stop constantly for rests.

Miss Uinne, the keeper, is at the door to meet us. We cross a large hall. There are coats of armour, tapestries and hunting scenes. Apparently, the asylum had once been the seat of the 12th Duke of Shitinhurst and had been open to the public three days a week. Today, visitors and coach tours still call at the house. They are shown no further than the Great Hall. Once, a party from Cunterferd Old Folks Club saw, by accident, some of the upper floors. Miss Uinne instructed that time-bombs should be placed in their charabanc. There were no survivors and the bodies were scattered among the privets and rhododendrons.

I am placed on a low table. The canvas is cut away and how wonderful it is to be able to see and breathe again. Mary, stiff and perplexed, refuses to leave the sack. She longs for a warm fire and a basket and a regular hot dinner. She is tiring of the scraps that I give her. Things like crisps, cheap cakes, chocolate and currant buns. She longs for proper meat.

Already, her coat is showing signs of malnutrition. Once glossy, it is now dull and grubby. Her eyes, that used to be so bright and sparkling, are now tired and hooded. And her paws are full of thorns, chippings and sores. Her collar, once so polished, is warped and cracked.

An aide summons us. We are led towards the lift. The sliding gates open and we step into the car. Could you press 5, please. Thank you. The aide leaves us and I am alone with Mary. We ascend. But between the third and fourth floors, the car stops. I press the fifth-floor button again. And again. Alarmed, I press the emergency bell. We do not budge. I shout and stamp my feet. In the distance, I hear passing feet—but they do not hear. Suddenly I hear someone sawing metal just above me. There is heavy breathing. Then a gasp. Someone is sawing the central control cable. There is nothing I can do. I clutch Mary. The lift falls 400 feet in five seconds—but suddenly a grappling cable jams and we land quietly. A terrifying experience. People run to the lift shaft and look down. A ladder is erected and we climb up. Mary is shaken but not hurt.

The inmates gather round us. Ghastly figures without proper form or construction. All excrete where they please; the place runs with it. Miss Uinne gave up house-training years ago. You cannot expect them to behave like humans. They were brought here in cages. This is not really living. The trouble is that they have long, long lives. Many here are well into their 100th year. On the ninth floor, we have a human sheep who remembers Disraeli. Look through that window. There's our burial ground.

An imbecile steps forward. He will show us to our room. Mary can sleep with me but must take her meals with the other dogs. The imbecile has difficulty in talking. He is a tragic case and is not allowed to see people in the outside world. Once, years ago, he was a champion bull who won prizes all over the country. But one night he got drunk and raped the farmer's wife. The farmer cast a spell on the bull and since that day he has been slowly growing the features of a human being.

On the way up, Bull gives us a brief guided tour. I see many strange sights. Wing E is crawling with caterpillars, mice, hedgehogs, ants, tortoises and snails. They are all chronic alcoholics. Poor things, they crave for sweet sherry as we pass.

I am not allowed to see Wing G. There are eight pad-locks on the door. Wing H is crammed with owls, bats, thrushes, rooks, oysters, mussels, moles and ewes. They are all violent sex offenders and must spend their days here. Each day, they are dosed with saltpetre. But fre-quently there are break-outs and havoc is caused in local villages. Wing K is full of rhinoceroses, vipers, gorillas, sharks, whales and geese. They are all violent and can-not be allowed to lead normal lives. Mary, inquisitive to see more, peers into a DANGER NO ENTRY room. Im-mediately, a shark snaps at her. She is winded but is oth-erwise alright. It will teach her a lesson. Bull asks if we would like to see the remaining wings. Politely, I refuse the invitation. I ask to be shown at once to my room.

The three other occupants of the room are already asleep. Women's underpants, brassieres and skirts are scat-tered across the floor. But the heads that protrude from the sheets are those of men. Suddenly I notice movement under the blankets. Two people are in the same bed. They are doing a strange sexual deviation involving flowerpots, silk pillows, chicken carcasses and milk bottles. Mary, suddenly excited, jumps onto the bed and asks if she could join in. I pull her off and scold her.

I find my bed and place Mary under the sheets. Miss Uinne knocks, enters and offers cocoa. Unable to sleep I gaze out of the window and study the burial ground in more detail. Bodies are sunk up to the waist in concrete. The top halves, decayed and stinking, stand erect. Miss Uinne says it is cheap, easy and entertaining.

I sleep soundly for three hours. But before it is light, I am woken by a loud banging that seems to shake the whole house. I run to the window and see a contractor's van and dozens of workmen with picks and shovels. There are trucks, cup-excavators and earth-moving machines. They are demolishing the asylum. I gather Mary and my few possessions and run into the corridor. Already other inmates are aware of the danger and run for the exits. There is panic and confusion. Whole walls cave in before my eyes and I see demolition workers move in with iron picks. Inmates, despairing of ever reaching the ground floor, jump from upper windows and die terrible deaths on the flagstones hundreds of feet below. I see Miss Uinne trying to comfort a fallen imbecile. His neck was broken. Carelessly, I trip on the body. Miss Uinne thinks I did it on purpose and punches my crotch. Suddenly the asylum's main staircase gives way. Hundreds sprawl. The demolition workers have orders to capture every imbecile. Nets are thrown and, outside the asylum, bulldozers are driven directly at them. Many try to hide, but are sought out by shotfire. There are terrible atrocities.

11

It is now 4.30 a.m. We have walked for hours along deserted country lanes. In the distance, we see the headlights of a long-distance bus. It is bound for London. We step in and tell the driver we will pay at the other end. He will not hear of it and threatens to throw us off the bus. Luckily, I notice the frills of women's underwear protruding above his blue serge trousers. So, confident that he is a pervert, I offer to go on the back seat and be dirty with him in lieu of payment. He agrees instantly and we pass a pleasant half hour in complete privacy. Unfortunately, the driver forgets to put on his knickers again and they flap about at the back of the bus. A senior police officer, travelling in the second back seat, spots them. The bus is stopped and we all have to get out and line up. We are ordered to drop our trousers. The driver, realizing the peril he was in, hid under his seat and refused to be inspected. So he was dragged off his bus and ordered to drop his trousers like the others. He refused and was instantly arrested. He faces serious vice charges. We had to wait two hours for a relief driver. The company made certain he was a married man.

It is a long, weary journey. Mary looks out of the window for some time, then tires and falls asleep beside me. The other passengers smoke and read newspapers, books and magazines.

N. L. Yinne, sitting in the third seat, taps the driver on the back and asks him to stop the coach. He is feeling sick. But the driver refuses. I am behind schedule. No one will mind if you do it out of the window. N. L. Yinne does as he is told and sticks his neck out into a gale-force wind on the A34. There is a throw-back and I get the whole lot in my face. It is the most extraordinary vomit. He must have a digestive disorder. In it, there are whole cutlets, rashers, burgers, sandwiches, sausages, pies and offals. Nothing is chewed. I go over and ask him to explain. He is embarrassed and refuses to answer.

To ease the tedium, I start to tell dirty jokes. Other passengers join in. Some are better than others. Suddenly, the driver turns round and says they are getting too dirty: Stop this filth, otherwise I must ask you to leave my bus.

In Market Street, Poulford, we are delayed by a large crowd outside St. John's Church. I shout to a passer-by and he tells me there has been an incident in the church. Apparently Roger Cooke is marrying Cynthia Rachel Charte. Guests were asked to be in their pews by ten-thirty and everything went according to plan until the procession. The organist played Bach's *Unititi Un Die* and the proud relatives turned their heads to the aisle. But the bride is not there. Something has gone wrong. Instead three men in black are carrying a coffin, followed by weeping parents. There has been a mistake. Vicar, what has happened? The whole congregation are in uproar and the Best Man runs to the pulpit. He addresses the people: I'm sorry. There has been an accident. The Vicar has made an error. He is not a machine. He thought this was a funeral service. A file had been muddled up or something . . . Then there was a delay and the ashamed Vicar ran from his church and drove his black van onto a lonely moor and stayed there till the fuss was calmed. The bride, tears pouring down her cheeks, ran from the church, did not see an oncoming bread-van and died under the wheels. At the Palace Hotel, Mr. Celinhi waits anxiously in his banqueting room. When he realizes the reception is cancelled, he throws 400 rolls down the lavatory and drinks 9 bottles of 13 and a half shilling Vive de Fuchenstein. He was found next morning under a sofa, and dismissed.

At twenty past twelve we stop at the Ace Pull-Up for lunch. There is a rush for the lavatory shack at the rear of the building. First come, first served. One at a time though. A queue of desperate-to-shit passengers stamp their feet. Many cannot wait and make no attempt to disguise the fact that they are excreting in public. I am well trained and wait patiently. At last my turn comes. The lavatory is in a filthy condition: rats, field-mice and carrion crows circle around outside the window. After excreting I am furious to find there is no paper. What can I do.

Luckily I see a newspaper seller across the road. I beckon him and, passing 5 pence out of the window, manage to get a *Morning Herald*. It serves my purpose quite adequately. Unfortunately it is a very cheaply printed local paper, and I am worried to find that my bottom is covered with newsprint that has come away from the paper. This dawdling means that the queue outside is getting angrier. Desperate knocks come every 30 seconds. Suddenly the door is flung open and a middle-aged man runs in with his trousers round his feet. He throws himself onto the bowl. I get myself off just in time.

I enter the cafeteria. It is terribly hot inside and the windows are steamed up. The proprietor, a huge man in overalls, stands behind the serving area. He holds a big scoop and is dishing out garden peas, rissoles and chips. There are 46 other passengers queuing in front of me. Suddenly the proprietor bangs a spoon. There is immediate silence. He announces that we are out of rissoles. There is no more food and no chance of more supplies till tomorrow. He says we must draw lots among ourselves to decide which passengers should offer his body. There is uproar. Men and women scream. But there is no alternative.

We must eat and someone must make their sacrifices. So, the lots are drawn. There is dead silence, the only sound coming from the washing-up machine. The proprietor is now holding up the selected name. It is Mr. K. P. Waite, a breakfast cereal salesman travelling to London. The proprietor approaches him, apologises and ties his hands and feet. Then he is taken into a back room, masked and shot through the head. There is a short pause and then we hear the mincer being turned on. Legs, arms and other limbs go in first. Very few of us dare to look. One passenger, shocked by this brutality, dials 999. In a few moments, I see blue flashing lights beyond the steamed-up windows. The inspectors run in and ask to speak to the proprietor. But rather than face them, he takes his own life.

It has been a rather dismal lunch and we return to the coach feeling down-hearted. After 20 minutes I fall asleep. I am woken a little later by a commotion coming from the front of the bus. One of the male passengers, a Mr. O. L. Pivve, is on the floor and trying to get his trousers off. Other passengers gather round. He is about to have a baby. In desperation, I ask if there is a midwife on the coach. Nobody comes forward so I assume responsibility. I get him on a double seat and remove obstructing garments. I tell him to keep his legs up. He groans and gasps. Other passengers crowd closer. I tell them to return at once to their seats. We are on a 4-lane motorway and the driver dare not stop. At last, with a great heave, he delivers a child. It is a boy and he names it Eric. Mary runs forward and licks away the afterbirth. She is good with children and you can trust them together. The Father is now buttoning his trousers. He smells like a drain and I do wish we could stop at the next services and wash him down. Suddenly I hear beastly chewing noises behind. Mary is trying to eat the baby. I grab her before it is too late.

Politely, I am asked to leave the coach with Mary. Otherwise we shall be thrown out of the window. I plead with the others. I promise that Mary will behave herself.

But they are adamant and, at Frampton Corner on the B34, we are once more standing on a windy verge.

Luckily, a passing vicar gives us a lift. He is travelling to London to lecture at a conference. We sit in the back of his red saloon. On the way to London, we stop at a laundrette. His surplice, now grey and stained, must be white by tonight. The assistant promises that it will be washed and dried in 20 minutes. We all wait in the car. Suddenly the laundrette manageress runs out of her shop and rushes towards us. She is in a wild panic. The vicar accompanies her back to the laundrette. There is a crowd gathered round one of the machines. It is the one that is washing the vicar's stuff. I push through and kneel beside the viewing-glass. To my horror, I see human limbs revolving amongst the surplice. The parson, tears pouring down his face, jumps into his car and drives away. I never saw him again.

12

I am in Cattel Street NW1 with no money, no hope and only the clothes I stand up in. I cannot go on very much longer like this. There is no way out. The daily strain is too much. Am sorry to be so dreary.

I walk to a telephone booth. Mary's mother is still alive and living in Charter St., SE1. The number is 222 6728. There is no answer but Mary says she is often out at this time. We go to the tube station. There is a commotion by the booking office. I see police and firemen. A lunatic had escaped from his handler and had stuck his penis in the automatic ticket machine. The firemen are trying to get it out. Ambulance men run with pads and morphine. The man is in agony. Nothing we can do.

There is a crowd on the platform. A dense crowd. Pickpockets are at work. They dip for wallets, jewels and bearer bonds. One is caught in the act and is chased down the platform. A station inspector closes all exits and the man is trapped. Unable to escape, he is driven onto the track by an angry crowd. Moments later I hear a train. The pickpocket scrambles desperately at the platform. But he cannot find a grip and falls back to face a terrible death. Blood spatters up against the tube, and the driver, white and shaking, faints into the hands of a station inspector. He is given three days off.

We are held up for two hours while ambulance men go down on the track. It is not pleasant work and several faint. Then firemen hose down the train. At last we are allowed to board.

Unfortunately the train stops in mid-tunnel between Charing Cross and Westminster. The guard speaks to us over his tannoy. Apparently the driver has abandoned the train and walked away up the tunnel. He had suddenly lost all interest in the job and had gone to take up a post as barman in a South London public house. Quickly, we gathered 300 signatures for a petition. Then someone runs up the dark tunnel and the driver is asked to return. He grudgingly agrees but drives badly to spite us, passing straight through several stations without stopping. Angry passengers run to the front of the train and knock on his separating window. They urge him to stop. He tells them all to fuck off.

Mary cannot quite remember the way from the tube station to her mother's house. We have to ask directions three times. At the corner of Cobb St., she is recognized by an old school friend. Where have you been all these years. But Mary is unfriendly and passes by without even a smile. She stops at the chemist and buys cosmetics and a brush. Can you put it on my mother's account? Your mother has left the neighbourhood, Mary. Didn't she write? I thought you would know. Yes, she has been at the Old Dogs' Home for over a year.

When Mary sees the house, tears well up in her eyes. There are boards over the windows and there is broken glass scattered about. The little front garden is overgrown with weeds and I see neighbours peering at us suspiciously. A rat runs up the basement steps. When he sees Mary he screams and runs down again. She tells him to get the hell out of it. Rat laughs and barricades himself in a tea-chest.

A taxi passes. I hail it and we jump in. The last passenger had been to the lavatory on the seat. I mention this to the driver and ask if he is going to take any action against the previous occupant. He turns round, scowls and says he did it himself. Why should I have to search for a convenience on a cold day like this. I am so disgusted that I only leave a penny tip. He is furious and tries to run us over.

13

THE DOGS' HOME IS A BIG WHITE BUILDING. OVER THE wall, I hear barks, wails, and growls. We ring three times. At last an attendant arrives. He is a disgusting man in an old serge uniform. Once, he told us he had been Head Keeper at a big Munich zoo. But he had been involved in an affair with one of his charges. A giraffe. He was instantly defrocked and this job was all that was offered. We were led to the administration office. The keeper opened a file and pulled out an index card. JOSEPHINE CLADIA RAMM, Dachshund. Born 10.4.17. Cell 6J. Admitted 8.11.69. The keeper asks us to follow him. Labradors, dalmations and terriers wander about the corridors. Nameless, they are lost and forgotten. An old pug named Jon whispers to me. He borrows 6 pence for a cup of tea. On each side I look into long 50-bed dormitories. Old bald-headed dogs lie asleep. There are gasping noises and uneaten trays of food. Spilt bed pans everywhere. I see a red setter having DTs on the end bed. I go over and hold his hand. There is vomit all over the sheets, and half a bottle of cheap wine hidden under the pillows. Under the bed there are many empty bottles of spirits. Years ago, he was owned by the late Lord Focle who drank himself to death. Red Setter was left to fend for himself and now, well into his 90th year, he seems to have adopted the habits of his former owner. He looks forward only to the few drops of alcohol that his miserable pension can afford. A sad dog. I wish I could do something.

A few beds away I can see a whippet lying very still. He is riddled with syphilis and barely alive. Dogs on each side of him do not give a fuck whether he gets medical care or not. He is at death's door. The priest is there but offering little comfort.

We return to the corridor. The Keeper shows us the

kitchen. I see the dogs' trays lined-up for the evening meal. Filth and grime is everywhere. The Head Cook, a crippled bull-dog named Sam, wanders about sticking his paw into boiling cauldrons. When he sees the Keeper he tries to hide. The assistant cook, a one-legged Siamese cat named Anne, runs forward and asks if we would like to sample the evening fare. I politely refuse. But she insists and gives me a helping. It appears to be a casserole of rats' heads. I try a mouthful and immediately vomit. A dear old sheepdog runs into the kitchen. He used to work for Sir Ivan Cutt's shepherd but is now too old and delicate. Sir Ivan sends the home £520 a year for his keep. He asks Anne if he might have his supper early as there is a telly programme he wants to see. Anne is furious and as a punishment makes him jump into an oven. He is baked for 20 minutes at Ratio 9. When he stops screaming Anne lets him out.

Now we are outside the Mother's room. The Keeper pushes open the door and lets Mary in. I feel out of place and decide not to enter yet. A moment later Mary runs out with tears pouring down her face. The Old Mother is dead. I rush in and see a small, stiff body on a sort of makeshift bed. The eyes are still and glazed. And the coat, once a fine reddish tan, is grey, lumpy and clammy. Long whiskers droop across her face. I should guess that she has been dead several days. The Keeper defends himself. It's not my business. I can't watch all of them. There's 300 dogs here you know. No you can't take her away. She'll have to be given to the cook for tomorrow's stew. You can't waste good meat.

Mary has broken down and is crying her eyes out. Other dogs from neighbouring rooms stand solemnly at the entrance. They realise and keep silent. I take the Old Mother and hide her in a rug. I try to clear up her possessions. On shelves, I see dentures, knitting needles, talcum powder, paperbacks.

As we leave, the Keeper runs forward with an envelope. It is a bill for £200. 18 weeks' keep. Today, I still receive solicitors' letters. They will sue.

The Mother will be cremated tomorrow at eleven. The owner of the cemetery rang today and said we must pay in advance. I ask Mary to dress appropriately. She must line her collar with black velvet and, if possible, wear some kind of a veil. She catches a 19 bus which will drop her outside a West End store.

14

Two hours later, the phone rang. It was the police. They had arrested Mary. She had been caught taking velvet from the haberdashery counter. The Store Detective had been watching her for 20 minutes and she had behaved suspiciously. Stunned and ashamed, I hurry to the police station. The duty sergeant says Mary will appear in court tomorrow morning. Till then, she must remain in custody. She had resisted arrest and tried to run for it. It is a serious offence. He adds that if I pay him £5 he will let Mary escape. But I haven't a penny on me. Look, would you like to be dirty with me? The policeman cannot make up his mind. He goes with women and has not had a homosexual experience since leaving school. But he is very tempted. I encourage him with details of positions etc. Suddenly with a nervous grin he agrees. We go down to the cells and he asks the gaoler to lock us both into number 17. Before we begin he sprays his already-stiff organ with fly-killer. I ask why. He says he saw a bluebottle crawling amongst his pubic roots just a few moments ago. During our disgraceful activities, I suddenly hear a key being put into the lock. We leap off the bed and grab trousers and underwear. The door opens and the gaoler puts in a Mr. K. O. Putte who has just been arrested for indecent exposure in a cinema off Old Street. What a lucky coincidence. All three of us get onto the bed and devise some entertaining positions.

Mr. K. O. Putte is evidently an expert and possesses tireless energy. Afterwards, I ask for details of his arrest. Apparently there had been an accident in the projection room. He had known the projectionist for some time and had called in between reels for some fun. Unfortunately, this afternoon, overcome with passion, they had knocked over the projector. Somehow their organs were coiled in the film and the image thrown on the screen. There was a gasp from the audience as Mary Yuller's *Laughter Game* was suddenly interrupted by a pair of throbbing organs. The manager, white with rage, dialled 999 and the police came and arrested both of them. It took three hours of intricate scissor and razor work to untangle the pubic hairs that had lodged themselves in the projector mechanism. Members of the audience were allowed to watch from the comfort of their seats. But when the projectionist's organ grew stiff from the prolonged untangling, the manager ordered the curtain to be dropped. A disappointed audience filed out.

Suddenly we are disturbed by a loud knock at the cell door. Again, we all rapidly button up trousers. The gaoler is outside with a man who occupied the cell last night. He thinks he has left his wallet under the bed. He comes in, nods at us and kneels down at the bed. He stretches, finds the wallet and stands up again. Unfortunately, while he was crouching, his organ slipped out through his buttons. We gather around and ask innumerable personal questions about exact length, volume, strength and velocity. The man is not amused and leaves the cell. A moment later, he returns and says he has changed his mind. I would like to do it with a man. I am sick of women. Any volunteers?

Later, the policeman, as promised, leads me to Mary's cell. She is bitterly upset about her crime and feels that she should face the justices tomorrow morning. I explain that she can now leave the police station. Thanking the policeman, we quickly leave.

15

I HAVE DIFFICULTY FINDING THE CREMATORIUM, AND AT one stage find myself on a No. 9 bus going totally in the wrong direction. I plead with the conductor but he refuses. I am forced to throw him off the bus and operate the STOP bell myself. He climbs back on and a fist-fight develops. Other passengers try to break it up. Stop it. Grow up both of you.

Mary, with a dog's sense of direction, eventually guides me to the correct address. But the crematorium gates are closed and I ring for 20 minutes before distant footsteps are heard. The attendant is sulky. He is not expecting us. There has been a clerical mistake. He says we must go away. But Mary's mother's body is at least 60 hours dead. We must do it today. So we push the attendant aside.

There are many paths in front of us. All stone-paved. We pass through rows of crosses, memorials, tombs, vaults, wreaths, pedestals and towers. The grass is overgrown; their gardener died three years ago and has not been replaced. With my sharp eyes, I see vipers, cobras and pythons sleeping or wandering amongst the tombs.

There is a long queue outside the crematorium building. All mourners with their deceased. Some humans, toads, bantams, rooks, pheasants, stoats and sheep. One crow has a hand-made coffin in polished oak. It cost £87. A toad has a tin cask. About £81 I think. Stoat cannot afford anything and has a paper bag. It is a strange sight. The priests circulate, collecting the money in advance. They do not take cheques. They do not have change for £5 notes. We mean to be as disagreeable as we can. Take your bodies elsewhere if you like. We don't mind.

Our turn comes. They want to know how we got past the gate-keeper. You're not on our list. Go to the back of our queue. We wait another half hour. It is terribly hot from the furnaces. Then Mary's mother is wheeled in. She is in an old sack and has been embalmed in a vague sort of way. I take one look and sign the identification form. Then the priest leads us to a viewing window. Thick plated glass. They ignite and I see the sack thrown in. I hide Mary's eyes but watch closely myself. Suddenly the fire dies. They have run out of fuel. Someone runs for twigs and twigling. But it will not light again, and there are further delays while a priest goes to the stores for fire-lighters. I watch him crawl into the furnace to insert them. It is terribly hot inside and he takes off his mantle. Suddenly there is an explosion. I lose sight of him behind huge flames. An hour later his remains are taken out. Hardly recognisable except for the copper medallion that hung round his neck. The other priests do not seem upset. It happens quite often. You have to be very careful. Dangerous work.

Then they put a scoop into the furnace and collect the Mother's half-burnt remains. A clerk comes forward and asks if I have paid. I fumble and say I have no money. Then we can't finish the cremation. I'm sorry. Those are the regulations. I plead with him and at last, after hours of begging, he gives us permission to bury the remains in the crematorium grounds. But he cannot complete the cremation. That is too expensive. Be careful not to disturb other graves. You will find an interment map on the way out. Don't waste my time.

I carry the charred bundle. Mary walks beside me. It is hard to find a vacant plot. Several times I dig and come upon bones and soft limbs after just a few feet. This interment map is not up to date. I return to the crematorium building and ask the clerk what he is playing at. He is having tea and is furious at being disturbed. But I insist and grudgingly he leads us to a plot that he believes to be vacant. We walk down a narrow path between laurels and come to a big grass area, at least the size of a tennis court. But there are people already there. Hundreds and hundreds of hens are lined up. Each carries a small bundle. I ask what happened. Apparently 500 chickens from Coddfird Friendly Society were taking a rail excursion to Clacton-on-Sea. There had been an accident. A collision with an oncoming goods train. Terrible slaughter and every chicken lost its life. The dependants have bagged the whole area for a mass burial. The clerk protests. Have you had permission. You can't just come along like this. There's a three-week waiting list. Immediately he is set upon by the angry hens. Some go for the neck. Some go for the eyes. He is down on his back in seconds and dead within the minute. Twelve minutes later all that is left are buttons, bones and shoes.

I am terribly cross with the hens. They cannot behave like this. Officials from the crematorium building, hearing the noise, run to the scene. When they see the bones of their colleague, they run for guns, hand-grenades, pikes and muskets. The hens, realizing that they are in danger, retreat behind a low wall. The first shots are fired and three hens fall. Twelve minutes later all 500 sprawl across the grass. Many are mortally wounded. Some walk a few steps then stumble and fall with blood issuing from wounds in throat, beak and breasts. The victorious crematorium officials move in to examine their kill. They choose two dozen of the plumpest birds for their own larder. That afternoon a buyer from a big local firm of poultry packers pays 2 pence each for the remainders. He leaves 36 behind. Too badly shot-up. Rooks, vultures and carrion-crows from local woods consume these unfit carcasses over the next few weeks.

We must get Mary's Mother buried. I ask a passing gardener and he directs me to a vacant plot near the greenhouse. The topsoil is undisturbed and I feel confident that we have at last found somewhere.

However, after digging 3 feet down, I hear shouts from below. We have discovered someone. I feel down with my hand and come across a human organ, very stiff. Then I grasp an arm and, with enormous effort, haul a Mr. J. P. Hinne up to the daylight. I ask him to explain himself. Apparently he had been having an affair with a badger. They had met at a fete. Badger had led him on and they did just about everything, apart from actual intercourse. J. P. Hinne, however, insisted on more and so, overcome with sexual ecstasy, he had even followed badger underground. When I discovered him, he was just about to slip in his organ. It is one of the most disgusting stories I have ever heard and I dial 999. Police come and, next day, he is sentenced to 25 years penal servitude. During that time he had no visits except from the after-care people. The Vicar of Deefel is interested in the case and may offer him work after release. It's nothing to laugh about and I'm thankful I prevented the matter going further. I am determined not to give up. A mourner passes and I ask if he knows of any vacant plot. He is extremely helpful and, seeing the Mother's corpse, offers deepest sympathy. Try that patch over there. The police exhumed someone last week. I don't think there's been a replacement. In the distance, I see an elderly man running to the same spot. He carries a dead terrier. I sprint for the last few yards and chase him away. Already flies, blue-bottles, scorpions and tarantulas are circling about. They swoop in turn and tread on the Mother's corpse. Go away you brutes. After descending 8 feet, my shovel collides with an iron man-hole cover. With Mary's help, I raise it and am astonished to find a huge dark cavern. We descend a rusted iron ladder, and, after 50 rungs, step onto a small ledge. There is a foul smell of piss and dung. We have accidently entered one of London's main sewers. Far above us I hear a clang. Someone has closed the manhole. We are trapped. We've lost the Mother's corpse for good. She'll get a pauper's funeral.

16

CAUTIOUSLY, WE CREEP ALONG A NARR-
ow shelf. It is hard to see and the sewer
gas makes breathing difficult. Mary
coughs continually. After a few moments we come upon a small canal.
There are rowing-boats tethered to the wall and two small
boathouses. We have no alternative but to steal a boat and
hope that our course leads us to dry land. I jump in and
give Mary the rudder. The water is thick with sewerage.
In the depths, I can make out toads, crocodiles and jumping sewer mice. Suddenly we are rocked by a great wave.
Stinking hot air is puffed into our faces and I feel turds
bumping against the boat. We have been joined by another tributary. In the distance, I see the advancing lights
of another boat. It is an inspection gang.

As they come closer, I am astonished to see that they
are not human beings. They appear to be giant rats with
claws as long as a man's arm. When they see us they shriek
with excitement and try to overturn our boat with stout
poles. Three jump aboard and jeer at me. Suddenly the
boat goes over and we are thrown into the water. Mary,
thankfully, holds on to me as we descend through thick
sewerage. The smell is indescribable and my legs are
caught up in lavatory paper. The water is approximately
the consistency of a cake before it is baked. I can't hold
my breath any longer. I take a mouthful of sewerage and
am violently sick. The rats, safe in their rowing-boat, glare
down and, believing us to be drowned, paddle quickly
away. Suddenly, I feel teeth bite into my thigh. It is the
sewer shark, a strange mammal that exists on excreta and
piss. He is quite harmless really and lets go when I stroke
his fins. Then a dreadful thing happens. I see a tiny child

float past me. No more than a month or so old. He is still alive and I lift him in my arms. It is a sad story. He was not wanted and had been flushed down the lavatory from a house in Ely Place, NW8. There was no money for his keep. The young couple had no alternative. They had tried everything. It's murder, of course. But the judge, when he heard the case, granted them a conditional discharge. The child is now a grown man and is working as a university professor.

With great effort, I manage to upright the boat and we climb in. After a few minutes, we hear a small voice calling from the waters. Mary leans over and I watch her bring aboard a half-drowned rainbow trout. She has a bizarre story to tell. A few months ago, a Mr. K. P. Lotte chose *truite au bleue* at the Rescini Restaurant in Buller Road. The maître d'hôtel scooped into the tank and this trout was unlucky enough to be chosen. She was then presented to K. P. Lotte for his approval. But K. P. Lotte is a very odd man with peculiar sexual habits. When he saw the trout, he immediately bought it and ordered the waiter to preserve it in a jam-jar. On no account was she to be cooked. That night he drove rapidly to his Mayfair penthouse with the trout sitting beside him in the Rolls-Royce. He rushed to his bedroom, threw Trout between the sheets, and took off his clothes. She was fucked and buggered in every possible position. Finally, totally exhausted, she was flung into a bathful of water to preserve her for the next night's activities. This brutal, senseless assault had continued nightly until today. With great difficulty, Trout had managed to raise the bath-plug. The next few minutes were terrifying. Travelling at over 50 miles per hour, she was thrust down miles of plumbing before arriving in the sewer. If we had not rescued her, she would have almost certainly drowned.

The sewer broadens here. Now it is a rushing torrent. Tributaries from hospitals, hotels and office blocks have joined. Everywhere, there is a dense mist of fart air. It is becoming more difficult to row and Mary takes one oar. The water is now the consistency of mashed potato. I catch a lavatory-paper manufacturer doing an inexcusable thing. He is propelling a small punt and collecting as much loose lavatory paper as he can find. When he has a basketful, he returns to his Islington factories, washes it, dries it and sells it again. He showed me one bit that had been round 18 times. There's money to be made. Try it yourself, my name's R. B. Tenne. A year later, I read in the paper that police had visited his factory, taken samples and arrested him. The judge sentenced him to 58 years hard labour. You are the most despicable human being ever to enter my court. I shall punish you with the utmost severity.

Round a corner, I come upon 20 or 30 frogmen. They appear to be searching for something. On the catwalk, I see a man directing operations with a megaphone. He is Sir Roland Humphrey. Last night he had been dining at Smith's, the Mayfair discotheque. His partner was a Miss Harriet Arsehole, the water-skiing champion. Unfortunately, during dinner, her £450,000 brooch fell into the soup. Humphrey swallowed it and did not realize his mistake until the following morning. Both were badly pissed-up and he had been to the lavatory a great many times during the night. With the greatest care, he now excreted into special aluminium panniers. The contents were thoroughly searched with the help of electro-magnets. But there was no trace. It must have passed through some time during the night. At great expense, he hired frogmen to search every inch of the main Fleet sewer. There had already been casualties. Two frogmen, after searching the floor of the sewer, had been unable to ascend through the dense sewerage and had perished. Already the sewer sharks have eaten the tenderest limbs. The other frogmen appear to be getting nowhere. Sir RH stamps his feet and urges more efficiency. He offers to treble their wages. But exhausted by the long ordeal, they give up. Sir RH, determined not to give in, slips out of his suit and dives in. I see him take a deep breath and descend. Two minutes later he rises and gives a triumphant cry. He has recovered the jewel. The frogmen crowd round to congratulate him. I watch the joyful party disappear in the distance. But they cannot find the exit hole. For hours they search. They are dizzy with fart fumes. Three days later, desperately hungry, they go down on their knees and scoop up excreta from the floor beneath them. It makes an unsavoury meal. But what alternative. Later, I hear that the sewer rats got them. There was a ritual killing near Potter's Bend. One of the rats is keeping the jewel for his little girl when she's grown up.

We press on. The current becomes swifter now and the rowing is easier. Six school children swim past us. They are learning the crawl. Their instructor, wearing a purple tracksuit, runs along the catwalk. They are from Cudlip Park Primary. Why d'you learn down here? Isn't there somewhere nicer? The instructor shakes his head and says that a bit of shit never did anybody any harm. Besides, he said, he had been banned from all public baths. I ask why and he tells me in the frankest terms. On April 18th, he was caught committing an obscene act with a 12-year-old. The Bath Attendant, himself a homosexual, said he would overlook the matter providing the instructor promised never to return. So he moved territories and, forging references, took a post at a small public school in Surrey. His duties were swimming instruction and part-time cricket instruction. Unfortunately, the head master caught him in a changing room being filthy with a boy named Dobson. The head master, himself an active homosexualist, gave the instructor one day's notice but otherwise overlooked the matter. Three weeks later, again with forged references, he took up a post at Medlinton Road Youth

Club as shower-room attendant. On the first Tuesday, the Administrator caught him trying to bugger a boy who was far too young to know anything about what was happening. The Administrator, himself a homosexualist with a long record of success with his youths, asked the instructor to leave. Nothing more would be said. By now, however, a Detective Sergeant Harris from Scotland Yard was catching up on the instructor. On the night of April 27th, he was arrested and taken to Pitt Street police station. Three weeks later, he faced Justice Cullum at the Old Bailey. Cullum, a kind and sensitive man, forgave the instructor all his sins and gave him an absolute discharge. But there was one condition. He ordered that the instructor's penis should be severed at the root. It would prevent any further trouble. The court is hushed and curious. The instructor is led onto a specially erected platform and asked to strip. Then a Mr. B. Z. Pinne, a police doctor, was called in to court. He carried Dettol, cotton wool, swabs and a pair of surgical clippers. The instructor is asked to kneel and the police doctor produces a set of dirty photographs. These are placed in front of him and immediately the penis rises. The doctor grabs it at the thickest part and deftly severs the organ. Bandages are applied and the instructor is led out of court. That night, he returns to the court and methodically searches the disposal bins. He finds his penis and, with amazing skill, re-fits it to his stump. Two years later it falls off in front of a large crowd. He is arrested on a gross indecency charge.

I am now anxious about leaving the sewer. Mary's cough is much worse. We cannot continue like this. I see a promising culvert and take a risk. It must lead somewhere. It is narrow and there is barely room for both of us. But the extra slime that adheres to the brick acts as a lubricant. We continue like this for about 60 yards until we come upon a sharp U-bend. The texture of the walls changes from red brick to vitreous enamel. We are just a few inches away from an ordinary, private-household toilet. Our only chance is to exit via the bowl. But suddenly we are disturbed by a long, resonant fart. Someone is using the lavatory. I squeeze further along and pray that Mary's weak shins can bear the pressure. My head is now in the base of the bowl. Above me, I see a vast white arse. It is a memorable moment. I wish I had a camera. A hand lowers with a wad of paper and on the other side I see a long dripping penis. He quickly wipes away surplus urine. I watch with great interest. He stands up, hoists ridiculously brief underpants and flushes. I hold my breath as the water passes over me. Then, to my horror, the householder glances down. White with rage, he slams down the lid and I am left in darkness. I hear him switch on an electric kettle. When it is boiling, he returns. I try to shield my eyes as he aims the spout directly onto me. I am badly burnt and cry out for him to stop. He shakes with rage and shouts abuse. He goes out of the room and returns with a huge copper cauldron. It is filled with boiling jam. The pain is excruciating and I receive first-degree burns. At 5.30 p.m., I pass out.

Four hours later, I regain consciousness. There is no sign of the man. Mary has worked herself loose and is licking my blisters with her soft tongue. When the firemen see me, they look grim and doubt my release. They chip for three hours with hand-axes. I am given hot soup and told to close my eyes.

17

I TRAVEL BY TAXI TO MY UNCLE'S HOUSE. AT THE CORNER of Hyde Street, I notice that there is a wasps' nest under the seat. They have seen me and hundreds are now flapping their wings. Apparently one wasp had been killed that morning by flying in front of a bus in Park Lane. The driver had tried to swerve but there was no hope. The wasps, angry and upset, will attend a memorial service tomorrow. One wasp named S. G. Hoode had written an obituary for insertion in *The Times*—but the Editor has just rung to say it is unacceptable. Illegible and badly constructed. You must do better than this.

I cannot pay the taxi. The driver has an effeminate profile so I decide to risk it. I'll show you my penis if you'll forget the fare. He seemed pleased and asked me to place my organ in his hand. He produced a magnifying glass and spent an  enjoyable two minutes. Then, to my annoyance, a wasp landed in my public hairs. He behaved extremely badly. First, he tied knots in many of my hairs. Second, he pissed and drenched all my crotch. Third, and most annoying of all, he gave me three bad stings. It was most painful and I was unable to have a comfortable erection for four days. The driver laughed. Serve you right you filthy fucker. Don't come in my cab again.

My uncle will not open the door. He shouts through the letter box. Come back in an hour. Curious, I peer through the window, and, beyond the curtains, I see my uncle lying across a sofa. A Mr. L. P. Yonne is uncoiling rope and winding it round my uncle's waist. Thongs are produced and 18 strokes are administered. L. P. Yonne takes off his suit and steps into size 8 velvet knickers. Up comes his penis and indescribable events follow.

I don't want to go on peeping at him like this. So I go round the corner to the Bull's Head and drink three pints. Unfortunately, Mary gets involved in a fight with the landlord's bulldog. There is a nasty scene. Bored regulars, anxious for drama, place both dogs on the bar and heavy bets are placed. The landlord, pissed and dribbling, bashes the arse of his dog with pale-ale bottles. He refuses to fight and jumps off the bar. The landlord is publicly disgraced by this cowardly performance and insists on making an example. He takes the bulldog by the scruff of his neck and slips his arse onto the best bitter nozzle. He pulls the pump and Bulldog screams. It is the most unpardonable piece of cruelty.

My uncle is waiting just inside the door. He is in a pathetic state. L. P. Yonne had panicked and run off, leaving whips, thongs and straps behind him. I dial 999 and ask for an ambulance. But when the drivers see my uncle, they shake their heads. We daren't help him. You'd better get him on the bed. I'm sorry. No perverts.

My uncle died that night. We waited up till 4 a.m. They did a post-mortem and a warrant is now out for L. P. Yonne's arrest. Police go as far as Edinburgh in the hunt and take over 200 statements. Finally he is traced to a poultry farm near Rochester. 40 police surround the area. Two armed inspectors enter the battery cage. It is ten o'clock at night and the 300 Sussex are asleep. They are furious at being disturbed and deny all knowledge of Yonne. But the police are not satisfied and search further. Each fowl is taken from its cage and questioned. Any fowl that refused to co-operate was punched in the face. Blankets were draped over one hutch and an inquisitive inspector tore them away. He discovered a cock having sexual intercourse with a young Rhode Island. Cock called out for a contraceptive; he had left his packet in the other hutch. Several of the hens were unable to leave their hutches. Either they were very pissed-up or very hung-over.

The disappointed detectives called off their search. L. P. Yonne had got away. But as they returned to their cars, they stumbled across a body. It was L. P. Yonne. He had been horribly gored by a bull. They said later that L. P. Yonne had tried to fuck Bull. No further proceedings necessary and the police leave. However, the farmer is furious with Bull and orders him to be chastised in front of his herd. There were pictures in all the farming press.

18

We lodge in my uncle's house. On the third day, the doorbell rings at eight in the morning. It is the postman with a registered letter for Mary. The Kennel Club of Great Britain have refused to renew her membership. You cannot go on like this. You are a disgrace to our society. Pull yourself together. Shocked and embarrassed, we go at once to the office. At the reception, a bulldog bars the way. Have you an appointment. I'm sorry, you can't just walk in like this. Major Oxley is a very busy man. Mary pleads and begs. Without the Kennel Club membership it is almost impossible to obtain decent employment. So we insist and at last the bulldog agrees. He leads us into the office and Oxley glares at us. Files are opened and a job in Compton Street is offered. £14 a week. Start next Monday. You will be in charge of the Jupiter Dirty Book Shop. Listen, Mary, don't let me down.

The shop has been empty for three months. Thieves had entered through an upper window and plundered the filthiest books. So we opened with no proper stock. On the first day, dirty book racketeers visited us and we bought 50 copies of Rudolph Cann's *The Vunvit*, and a large assortment of dirty pictures. We opened on Tuesday March 16th and took £165 in the first two hours. However, at eleven o'clock, I saw a police car draw up. They took away stock and asked if we had any dirty pictures. I show them into the back room and they search at random. Without them seeing, I throw the 'hedgehog in bed with young girl' into the lavatory bowl and flush. The police realize what I have done and run out to their car for the official Police Cod. He is carried in, still in his tank, and tossed down the U-bend. At first he refuses to submerge but the police threaten and he is obliged to do his duty. He does not return after four minutes and the police get worried. He cost £300 to train and cannot be lost like this. They call his name and whistle. But no sign, and after 20 minutes he is presumed drowned. The police leave us. One officer, a man younger than the rest, holds back. He hands me a dirty book he has written and wonders if I would like to publish it. Thanking him, I go into the back room for a quick glance. I'm afraid I had to return it. Too many four-lettered words. 'Fuck' came up 350 times in the first paragraph. It is ridiculous and sordid. There were crude illustrations that he had drawn himself. Huge penises and vaginas completely out of proportion. We can't possibly sell this. I'm so sorry.

Next day, there was another visit from the police. All senior men. They knelt beside my toilet. You've killed our cod. We'll say prayers now. Inspector Snaith, who had cared for the cod since it was a small child, wept openly. Then, to my astonishment, bubbles began to appear on the surface of the water. A moment later, the cod rose, gasping for air. Inspector Snaith, tears pouring down his face, held Cod in his arms. It can't be true. My cod has come back to me. All of you, go away. I want to be alone.

A week later, they closed our shop. Four police stand outside and they have hung curtains over the windows. The books are being taken away in an old hand-cart. They have been bought by a clergyman who made a million out of sermon ideas. His name is Rev. Frampte. Today I learn that he has bought the site, destroyed the shop and is now building a church. Each day he takes a collection in the street. He must have £10,000 by summer. Otherwise the site will be lost. I do all I can to help. There are stained-glass windows to be sketched and carpets to be woven. Silversmiths come from Asia and Peru with goblets, crosses and sculpture. On April 28th the roof is erected and Rev. Frampte flies to New Orleans to collect rare surplices and choir-boy cassocks. Today, the men from Harrisons work for 12 hours on organ tubes. Pitch cannot be faulty. They are casting the bells now at a small foundry in Bath. Four 8-ton E-flats with one antique F cast before the Reformation. An appeal for kennels. 500 must be ready by August 1st.

On July 22nd, Frampte stopped me in the street with tears in his eyes. There were no more funds. I can't possibly finish the church. Look, those men over there are creditors from a church fabric factory. And, next to them, sitting in that saloon, is a man from Howarth's Debt Collection Service. It's £480 owing for altar furnishings. They're all essentials.

That night I go with Mary to the Art Gallery in Bouth Square. I take away a lower pane and step in. Immediately, the alarm rings and four patrols run for me. However, they are too pissed-up to really know what has happened. I pretend to be Eugène Delacroix returning to claim a work which is not really their property. They accept this explanation and show me to Room 15. There are several fine Delacroix there and I choose two. They fit nicely into my attaché case. As I leave by the main door another alarm bell is set off in the Director of the Gallery's Islington home. Luckily he is just about to bugger a friend and cannot be bothered to attend to it.

The pawnbroker gave me £10,000. This was more than enough and all debts are paid. On the following Tuesday, police visit the church. They are enquiring about the stolen Delacroix. We claim sanctuary and run to the High Altar. They are furious and fetch tear gas and smoke

bombs. But we do not budge and, after 12 hours, they drop the charge.

At eleven o'clock that night, the Anglican Archbishop rings from his palace. He cannot undertake the consecration. You must find another church. I don't want to have any more to do with you. Desperate, the vicar tries Rome. But the Vatican is not interested and hangs up. We try Quakerism, Methodists, Wesleyans and Christian Scientists. They are not interested either.

The vicar, overcome with grief, goes to the vestry and drinks two bottles of altar wine. Then he jumps into his saloon and drives up the M1. Near Exit 11, he intentionally drives across the central reserve and collides with an oncoming diesel. He dies in the ambulance and is given a pauper's funeral in a Salvation Army graveyard. There are gravediggers' fees of 1 shilling. I cannot pay them and watch helplessly as they immediately tear away turf that they have only just laid. No fees, no burial. I'm sorry—that's the way things are nowadays. You'll have to bury him yourself.

19

I QUEUE TO SEE MR. FICCE AT THE KENNEL CLUB. EIGHT in front of us, all after the same job. Hacton Bishop, the big West Country dog-food manufacturers, are looking for a new dog-food taster. One of their senior tasters, a terrier named Jackson, has lost his life in an exploding boiler incident.

Mary is still in doubt. I insist and promise to accompany her to the interview. The Kennel Club kindly charter a four-seater Heron. We must be at the airport by two o'clock. While I wait on the tarmac, a nasty incident occurs. I am struck on the head by several pieces of hard turd. They appear to have fallen from an aircraft passing overhead. Three weeks later, I receive a long letter of apology from the captain. He said there had been a leak in the stools tank. I'm most frightfully sorry. It's never happened before. Do please send dry-cleaning bills.

Then the pilot appeared. He asked if I had ever flown before. Can you please keep silent during flight. This will be my first solo flight. I left flying school only last week.

Shaking with fear, I entered the aircraft with Mary in my arms. The pilot seated himself and tried to warm up the engines. There don't seem to be any seats for us. An empty box and three cushions. Look, this isn't good enough; you must provide proper seating. But we were already moving along the runway. I saw the pilot groping for the correct levers. He constantly made errors and we swerved, braked and shook. When we were several hundred feet up, he turned to me and said he had forgotten what to do next. Poor man, he had spent a penny in his pants. Shock, I suppose. I search for an instruction booklet. In the back portion of the plane I am horrified to find the remains of an air hostess. Skeleton and metal badges left. She was bent over her chair. Years ago, the aircraft had been used for military transport. And one day she had locked her door, fainted and been forgotten. That night I placed the remains in a stout bag and sent them, cash on delivery, to the Air Ministry. They did not want to know and threw bag and bones out of the window.

We are 900 feet over Icley Common and the pilot is urging me to help. We are losing height and must pull ourselves together, otherwise we face certain death. The little aircraft splutters and coughs. We are out of fuel. Why the fuck didn't you fill up before we left. Then, to my horror, I see a propellor dropping off. It lands outside a supermarket in Icley High Street. Three housewives suffer grievous wounds. Aren't there any parachutes. I'm sorry, I forgot to put them in. I'm frightfully sorry.

Suddenly, Mary tugs at my cuff. A rook has settled on the wing. He seems friendly and, in seconds, his quick brain has grasped our plight. With great haste, he departs in the direction of a nearby rookery and returns in three minutes with 800 rooks. They settle themselves on wings, fuselage and nose. They flap like hell and keep us up until we are in sight of the airport. I can't thank you enough. You've saved our lives. Is there anything I can do in return.

Head Rook looks at me keenly and tells a sad story. Apparently the Earl of Fuck, who owns their rookery, is fed up with them and next weekend is arranging a house party to shoot them all dead. Is there anything you could do?

20

I HAD A HOMOSEXUAL AFFAIR WITH LORD FUCK AT SCHOOL and know him well enough to telephone. Yes, that's right. We're going to blast those fucking rooks to pieces next weekend. I've got a big party coming. There's Nicky Shit, Lord 'Arsehole' Drew, Rory Scott . . . bring a gun and join us. Come in time for dinner.

Head Rook, though terrified by the news, is determined to resist. He gathers his flock and they return at once to their rookery. En route, they stop at the gunsmiths and purchase 2.2s, shot-guns, grenades, daggers, explosives and other weapons. For three days they practice manoeuvres, defence drills. They are meticulously soldiered by Head Rook. On the Friday evening, they climb their trees and take up positions. Nicky Shit and Lord 'Arsehole' arrive in a small sports car. (Their faces are flushed: I would guess they have been abusing themselves during the tiring Friday evening journey.)

A little later, other members of the house party arrive. All get very drunk at dinner and, at twenty to three, many piss into their glasses.

Next morning, they set out in the direction of the rookery. Assistant Rook gives the alarm and all take up their appointed positions. Robins, doves, thrushes and pigeons gather in neighbouring elms. They have heard the news and watch eagerly. Lord Fuck fires the first shot; he is too badly hung-over and misses. Then Nicky Shit raises his shot-gun and sends 400 pellets up into the branches. A junior rook cries, twists and falls 400 feet. The labrador takes her carcass to the mortuary. Now Head Rook retaliates. He aims directly at Nicky Shit's heart and fires. He's crumpling and down on his knees. Blood pouring from a deep wound. Labrador drags him away. There's a loud

cheer of encouragement from watching birds. Lord Drew's turn. This expert shot scores a direct hit and Assistant Rook dies instantly. Lord Drew fires again and another junior rook falls. She's not badly hurt, just a broken wing. But she is captured and mercilessly tortured. They want information about the rooks' weapon source. How many other rooks are up there. Which rook was responsible for shooting Nicky Shit. But brave junior rook lowers her head and refuses questions. They are furious and pull her wings. She is in agony and sweat pours off. Then Lord Fuck produces a pen-knife from his pocket and slowly cuts off a claw. This pain will cease if you'll betray your friends. She shook her head. They lose patience, throw her to the ground and stamp on her. Labrador protests. That's awful. You can't behave like this. Immediately Lord Fuck kicks Labrador in the ribs. Whose side are you on?

Head Rook, enraged by this cruelty, throws a hand-grenade at Lord Drew. It lands in his pocket. He tries to get at it but too late. He is split in half and all his bowels come out.

Head Rook orders his staff to retreat. They climb further into the trees and try to disguise themselves in the foliage. An assistant throws a hand-grenade at Rory Scott. It lands at his feet and explodes instantly. He is blown to pieces. Now game-keepers are running to the rookery. They carry heavy rifles and are ordered to shoot all rooks dead. Head Rook is determined not to surrender and orders his rooks to keep their heads down and aim for Lord Fuck. A sharp-eyed junior rook scores a direct hit on one of Lord Fuck's testicles. Sperm pours out and every rook laughs. Lord Fuck is furious and orders his game-keepers to set fire to the tree. There is a pitiful screaming as the poor, brave rooks are suffocated by dense smoke. They fall into broad nets held by waiting game-keepers. However, one Senior Rook manages to slip into a mask and remain conscious. Single-handed, he resists for a further 20 minutes and hurls stones, shit and hand-grenades at Lord Fuck and his men. Finally, he collapses with exhaustion and falls to the ground. Lord Fuck, unable to control his anger, kicks at him until the skull cracks in several places.

At four in the afternoon, Lord Fuck's cook, Miss Grieve, is busy preparing an enormous rook pie. Lord Dob is coming over from Skelton with a party of ten: there must be no mistakes. She uses the finest ingredients: expensive hand-ground flour from a local mill, carrots from the home farm and mushrooms flown in from Dijon that morning. Miss Grieve has won many international competitions for her pastry, and her celebrated Coinou de Finne won the Golden Bowl at the Salon Culinaire in Paris last summer. The estate poulterer has already plucked and gutted the rooks. Eighteen carcasses wait for Miss Grieve's attention on a wooden board. She sets the oven to Ratio 6, places rooks, stock and vegetables into a pot and covers with pastry. Then she reads a woman's paper for twenty minutes. Suddenly she is disturbed by a moaning from inside the oven. She opens the door and sees a rook trying to push his way through the pastry. He has cleverly avoided the poulterer's deft hands; he carries a pistol and appears to be in a furious temper. Before Miss Grieve has a chance to raise the alarm, he has jumped out of the oven and pointed his gun at her. Stay where you are. Don't move or I'll shoot. Rook jumps to the sink and runs the cold tap: he is trying to get off the gravy that matts down his feathers. Rook then leaves the kitchen. He flies cautiously to the library. Lord Fuck is reading *Country Life* in a deep leather chair. Rook aims, fires and Lord Fuck falls forward. Severe face laceration, brain haemorrhage and other grievous injuries. He dies in just over a minute.

Then Rook gives a signal. Immediately other birds enter through the open French windows. There are giant eagles, carrion crows, vultures and other large species. In 20 minutes, they have completely dismembered Lord Fuck's body. Every limb is sorted and neatly stacked. Then Rook produces a knife. He shaves off edible flesh from wrists, thighs and chest. This is taken to the kitchen and Miss Grieve is forced, at gun-point, to add it to the pie.

That night, Rook returns alone to his tree. Depression soon sets in. He is desperately lonely without the other rooks and, some time during the night, he throws himself off a branch. He is found by woodsmen and buried in the Animal Graveyard. But when Lord Fuck's heir hears of Rook's foul deeds, he orders the body to be exhumed and thrown to the dogs.

21

OUR AEROPLANE HAS BEEN REPAIRED AND REFUELLED, AND we are once more moving along the runway. After we have been airborne for about ten minutes, I hear the public address system being switched on. The pilot tells us that we are about to crash-land. He has a choice of a ploughed field, an arable pasture with grazing Friesians or a school football-pitch with game in progress. An impossible decision: ploughed field would mean buckled undercarriage and possible explosion; arable pasture is almost suicidal—too many Friesians about to obstruct. Only real choice is the playing-field. But young boys in the prime of life could lose limbs and possibly life.

We fasten safety belts and grip seats. Mary's heart beats fast: we are going for the football pitch. I see the pilot switch on a hazard warning horn. Just a hundred feet below, I see the horrified games-master blowing his whistle. Run boys, run for your lives. But many do not hear, they are too involved in the game. I see the pilot close his eyes and cover his face. Now the games-master is running just a few yards in front of the left propel-lor. Then, unaccountably, he trips and falls. The propel-ler catches the seam of his flannel jacket. He is thrown up, sliced and taken to bits. The blood splashes on my viewing window. (I must try to stop his wife identify-ing him.) We've touched down now. Boys are tumbling about by the undercarriage. Games shorts are shredded and many boys lose their lives. Staff run from the school house, but they've only got one first aid kit to tend the 23 wounded. I hear ambulances trying to get along narrow lanes. There's a herd of bullocks blocking the entrance to the field and the drivers go frantic. They abandon their vehicles and run across three fields with stretchers under their arms. The bullocks, annoyed at the noise and interruption, charge at them. They shield themselves with stretchers. The pilot, unable to face the terrible responsibility, has jumped into a propellor. Poor soul, the extrication takes hours and we call urgently for aeronautical mechanics. Through the schoolhouse window, I see the head master on the phone. Judging by his pale face, I should guess he is telling next-of-kin. There is a list of deceased in front of him.

After walking some distance along muddy lanes, we are pleased to see a refuse truck pulling up in front of us. The dustbin men ask if we want a lift. You'll have to sit on the refuse in the hopper. They help us up and I sit on what seems to be a good place. All around me are large rats. It is not very pleasant. They continually try to make conversation. Where've you come from? Where are you going? Every so often, the truck stops and more refuse is thrown in. Each binful seems to have at least two fat rats. They all know each other and chatter incessantly. Mary, tired by recent events, is trying to get to sleep on my lap. Suddenly she loses her temper and tells one particularly loud-mouthed rat to shut his fucking trap. He takes violent offence and confers with the other rats. They mutter and whisper. Then with no warning they go for her. I fight them off with the jagged edges of empty tins, but Mary is badly shaken and afraid to travel further in the truck. At the next stop, we jump out.

We are still some 5 miles from the dog-food factory and there is no transport. A passing doctor offers us a lift to the factory gates. He is an interesting, friendly man and tells us his history. Years ago he had been a famous neuro-surgeon earning thousands of pounds a year. Unfortunately, one day he had arrived drunk for an important operation. He had bungled it and offered his resignation.

22

MR. SIMME IS WAITING FOR US IN THE RECEPTION. HE IS manager of the Pet Food Company and wants to know why we are so late. Follow me, you'll share a dormitory with the other tasters. We pass through the factory and see the steaming aluminium cauldrons and strange canning apparatus. There is a smell of burnt fat. Mary hasn't eaten properly for some time and snatches a piece of meat from

 a bin. Mr. Simme sees and orders her to replace it. How dare you behave like this. As Mary returns the meat, I am astonished to notice that it appears to be part of a man's wrist. Mr. Simme, realising that I have noticed, takes me aside and asks me to mention this to nobody.

The dormitory is dark and poorly ventilated. I can make out the shapes of other tasters asleep in their beds. One or two are still awake; they look up and glare. I am the only human in the room. A badger appears and introduces himself as the Head Taster. He shows us to our beds. To my annoyance, I find the body of my predecessor still between the sheets. We try to roll him off but are beaten back by a number of angry maggots that are nesting in him. Other tasters, woken by the disturbance, crowd round and offer assistance. We raise the corpse and dispose of it through the proper channels. I borrow some blankets from a neighbouring taster and, with Mary safely in my arms, fall at once into a deep sleep.

At ten past two in the morning I am woken by someone sitting on my bed. It is another taster. He asks if he can fuck me. I accept immediately and raise the sheets for him to enter. But as he climbs in, he clumsily hits Mary on the chin. She is livid and snaps at his organ. Stupid dog, she takes it right off at the roots and he screams with pain. Drop it, Mary. Drop it.

I have not made a very good start and next morning Mr. Simme is waiting for me. Apparently your dog attacked one of the tasters during the night. This isn't good enough. You must both pull yourselves together. Come on, I'll explain your duties. We are led once more through the factory. Coloured women are ladling boiled meat into cans. Beyond them, I see an enormous hopper. It is loaded with what appears to be human limbs. Anxious, I call Mr. Simme for an explanation. He is sullen, rude and afraid. Mind your own business. I watch him cover the hopper with a stout tarpaulin. Then the foreman appears. He shows us how to can the meat. You must be careful not to fill them too full. Most canners do 70 an hour. You should manage at least 100. I tell the foreman I am going to spend a penny. I return at once to the hopper, raise the tarpaulin and peer over. It is a revolting, sickening sight. The nude bodies of at least 80 humans are piled on top of one another. And at the base of the hopper I can see a huge mincer grinding limbs and bones. A covered conveyor-belt transports these hideous remains to the preparation area where workers, unaware of what they are handling, slice and prepare the meat for canning. I am horrified and am about to be sick when a firm hand grasps my waist. It is Mr. Simme. He is speechless and drags me to his office. I am asked to strip and place my clothes in a small linen bag. I refuse, and he kicks me in the balls. Who is your next-of-kin? He puts me across his shoulder and carries me, like a naughty child, towards the hopper.

I scream and plead for mercy. Thankfully, Mary's sharp ears pick up my distress calls. She puts down what she is doing and runs as fast as her four legs can carry her. She is just in time and, with characteristic accuracy, goes for Mr. Simme's most sensitive spot.

He falls forward, clutching himself, and as his grasp

weakens I throw myself clear of the murderous hopper. Workers crowd round and, in the distance, I hear police sirens. Mr. Simme, realising the game is up, starts to run to his office for cover. Now police officers are running across the factory floor. We just see Simme disappearing round a corner and by the time we are at his door, he has already locked himself in. A senior police officer is writing out a warrant for his arrest and others are knocking sharply on the door. It will be better for you if you come out quietly. Don't try any funny business. Beyond the door, I hear Simme sharpening a razor. Then blood begins to seep from the other side. Simme has taken his own life. He could not take his punishment like a man. Do what you like but be prepared to pay for it. They take away his body. He died intestate. Many charges were brought against other members of the company. Several, unable to face justice, jumped into the hopper and lost their lives. But most of them are now serving long sentences in lonely cells.

23

In order to raise the rail fares home, I do three hours' gardening for a man called L. P. Toote. He is a retired army officer and meticulous. I am given a hoe, a fork and a wheel-barrow. For the first hour he watches me from an upper window and gives instructions and warnings over a hand megaphone. Mind that hydrangea. Watch out, you're going to step on my bietiunium. Take more care. Look, you've missed out one bit . . . At last he ceases and I am left to myself. It is a pleasant, well-planned garden and time passes quickly. By eleven o'clock I have finished almost all the weeding and am just about to stop when my hoe hits something under the soil. I kneel down to examine and am astonished to find that I have discovered a human leg. Cautiously, I prod it with my hoe and realise it is not just a leg but a whole body. It is badly decayed and is teeming with maggots. I drop my hoe and run into the house. I dial 999 and urge them to come at once. In three minutes, I hear sirens coming up the drive. Then, upstairs, I hear feet run across a room. It is Brigadier Toote and he is panicking. He runs around in circles, shouting and swearing. Then he rushes downstairs and across the lawn, and tries desperately to replace the body. But the police are too quick and he is arrested, cautioned and taken to the police station. However, the police are too hasty and cross a red light. A school bus cannot stop in time and there is a collision. Brigadier Toote is thrown through the windscreen and dies instantly. The driver and inspector suffer grievous wounds and spend the rest of their days in the Police Rest Home at Bodmin.

The journey back to London is dreary and fraught with difficulties. I stop constantly at phone-boxes and make reverse charge calls to the Kennel Club, but they refuse to accept them and replace the receiver. Near Ratford-on-Avon, a passing vet pulls up and lowers the driver's side window. Your dog is in a shocking condition, she's in no fit state to be walking to London . . . He insists on giving Mary an immediate examination at his surgery in the local town. I am not unduly worried. She has coped remarkably well over the past difficult weeks and, apart from exhaustion and grime, there is not much wrong with her. The vet becomes offensive and asks me to leave the surgery. Would you mind going into the waiting-room? I'd much rather look at her alone. I settle in the end chair and read magazines. After a few moments I am disturbed by a down-and-out bulldog with a septic foot. He wants to borrow 6 pence for a cup of tea. I give him all I have and he stumps off without a word of thanks. I call him back. He gets nasty and threatens to beat me up. I apologise, give him my tie and tell him to forget the whole thing.

The vet comes into the waiting-room. Mary is under his arm. She is weeping. He calls me into the surgery, and, with a grave voice, tells me that Mary is 4 months pregnant. I snatch her from him and run out into the street. We walk silently towards a nearby park and settle on a vacant bench. She gasps and sobs. I do my best to comfort her. Why didn't you tell me? I could have helped. Mary hangs her head and says she has not had a period since she met me. Who was it? Was it your terrier friend? Mary begins to cry again and it becomes difficult to learn the tragic story.

She tries hard to explain. One night, not long before we met, she had accepted an invitation from a terrier named Ivan. They went to see *One Night in Cairo* at the Odeon and then went to the Ristorante Xcvuzilty for a quiet dinner together. After paying the bill, Ivan asked if Mary would like to come back to his room for coffee. Politely, Mary said no. But Ivan insisted and, against her will, he dragged Mary back to his room. He threw her on his bed, pulled out his penis and forcibly raped her. At two in the morning, Ivan fell asleep, exhausted by his activities. Mary crept out and made her way to the police station to report the crime. But the constable on duty was not interested and asked her to leave. I offer my deepest sympathy. It would have been a terrible experience for any dog, but for someone as sensitive as Mary it must have been especially nasty.

The pain of having to tell this hideous story made Mary break down again and weep openly. A sparrow, who had been circling for a few minutes, settled on our bench and asked if he could do anything. He went close to Mary and wiped away the tears. Don't worry my dear. You're in kind hands now . . . But Mary, bitterly ashamed, jumped off the bench and disappeared. I chased after her, afraid she might come to some harm. Sparrow, still anxious to help, offered to search from the sky. He was most efficient and called in pigeons, chaffinches and robins to help. Find the little brown dachshund. She may try to take her life. She answers to Mary.

After half an hour, Sparrow returned in wild excitement. Quickly come to the pond. Mary has hired a paddle-boat and threatens to jump off in the deepest part. Sparrow gives me a ride and we soar over trees and bushes and reach the pond in a few minutes. Crowds are gathered all around the banks and ambulance men are ready with respiration equipment. I throw off my clothes and swim furiously to the boat. As I get nearer, I can see her little body perched right on the bows. She is shivering and leaning over. I shout and call her name.

She is about to jump. Mary, Mary, don't be a fool. There is still another 20 yards to swim and I am losing strength. Sparrow flies just above me, urging me on. Other birds are there too, ready to do whatever is necessary. Then, when I am not more than 5 yards away, Mary jumps. For a moment she splashes desperately and I think she's going to keep herself up. But she's lost all strength lately and I watch helplessly as her head sinks below the surface. Tears are pouring down Sparrow's face. He has tried so hard to help and can now do no more. I take a deep breath and dive down as best I can. One fathom down, I make out her body. She is spinning and death can't be far away. I try to clutch her. Luckily, a friendly pike passes. He flaps his fins and asks if there is anything he can do. I cannot hold my breath any longer and ask Pike to continue the pursuit. This strong, experienced fish has no difficulty in catching up with Mary and he returns to the surface with her clasped firmly in his arms. I thank him warmly and take Mary onto the boat. She is frightened, shaken and upset. Then I notice that Pike is still hovering. There is a disagreeable expression on his face; I think he expects a tip. But I have nothing to give and tell him so. He takes offence and threatens to upset the boat if I do not reward him. There is a nasty scene which does nothing to improve Mary's poor condition.

Sadly, I row ashore and try to hide Mary from the onlookers and press photographers. The ambulance men are disappointed and drive grumpily home. We are alone now; the crowd do not linger when they realize there has been no catastrophe. Far out in the water, I can still see Pike. He is still furious. The birds, bored by the anticlimax, have departed to their nests. Only faithful Sparrow remains. He swoops low over us and asks again if there is anything he can do. I take him on my shoulder and together we walk to an open-air café.

The proprietor brings three teas and a towel. I dry Mary as best I can and pour tea into a saucer for her to drink. Sparrow asks if he might have a buttered bun. I ask for it at once. It is small reward for all he has done for us. He tells me a bit about himself and it turns out to be a sad story. His wife and three children were dead. There had been a tragedy. A roadside elm in which they were nesting had been struck down in a motor accident. It was two in the morning and the charabanc driver had been drinking. 14 old people lost their lives and the driver spent 18 months in hospital. Sparrow, realising that the charabanc was on a collision course, tried desperately to wake the family. Too late, their nest was thrown to the ground and Sparrow alone managed to throw himself clear. Today he is still homeless and is living a wretched existence in a chimney pot. It is wet, cold and lonely. And whenever the inhabitants below light their fire, he has to clear out for fear of being smoked alive.

Though burdened by his own problems, he sympathises keenly with Mary's plight. He writes down the addresses of several good abortionists in London and offers to put us up for the night if we would prefer to make the journey tomorrow. As it is now late in the evening we accept eagerly and set off at once for his chimney. On the way, Sparrow is involved in an incident with a crow. Apparently Sparrow owes crow seven pence and crow wants it back. I shoo the crow away, telling him to grow up and not be so fussy over such a small sum. (Crow is a well-known local miser and is reputed to own over 37 nests.)

We stop at the Bull's Head which is just a street away from Sparrow's chimney. Mary drinks large whiskies and gets pissed-up rather quickly; I think she is trying to drown her sorrows. After half an hour she gets noisy and the landlord asks her to leave. She refuses and orders another double large whisky.

The landlord loses his temper and orders his labrador to kick her out. A row develops and Mary gets a cut lip. It is unpleasant, unnecessary and thoroughly embarrassing. I apologise to the landlord on Mary's behalf and we leave immediately.

Sparrow is impatient for us to see his chimney. But Mary stops once again and insists on ordering herself a large whisky at the Cock Tavern. I ask the landlord not to serve her: she has had enough. Mary, for the first time since we met, turns on me and tells me to mind my own business. Before she has a chance to bite, I muzzle her teeth and take her into my arms. She scowls and struggles, and, as we leave the pub, she is violently sick all over my coat. Then she passes out. Sparrow jumps down onto my shoulder and points to a tall chimney stack. The inhabitants of the house are in—we have to climb carefully. The ascent would have been difficult enough without Mary, but with her it is most difficult and I nearly topple twice. We pass along a narrow ledge just above an attic window. A light is on and I see a couple having sexual intercourse. It is most interesting and I halt for a moment to watch. But Sparrow, anxious to get everything settled, urges me on. I move off too quickly and send a slate crashing down. The startled couple leap off the bed, fearing they have been discovered. Unfortunately, the male withdrew too quickly and his penis snaps off. He howls with pain and I feel awkward and embarrassed.

Sparrow flies ahead and prepares the chimney for his two new lodgers. Generously he vacates his own bed and says he will be quite alright elsewhere. It is a snug little place, just on the ledge where the stack meets the flue. He offers us his pyjamas and says he will bring extra blankets if we are cold. Mary begins to splutter and, afraid that she is about to vomit again, I ask Sparrow to bring a bowl. He brings me one, then waves good-bye. I'll be sleeping in the next-door chimney. Don't hesitate to call me if there's anything you need. Breakfast is a moveable feast. I'll wake you at eight.

At three in the morning, I wake suddenly from a deep sleep. The inhabitants below have lit their fire and smoke puffs all around. I can hardly breathe. We must get out quickly before the fumes overcome us. Mary, still drunk, refuses to get up and tells me to fuck off. So I drop her in a pillowcase and carry her over my shoulder. She growls and snarls and asks what the hell's happening. But it is the only thing to do. Sparrow, realising the danger, is panicking at the top of the chimney. He urges us to hurry, lest we suffocate from the horrible fumes. Unfortunately, just as I am scrambling out of the chimney, the pillowcase splits and Mary falls through the bottom. There is a frightful cry as she falls 20 feet down the flue. Sparrow, with great presence of mind, swoops to street level and taps furiously on the window pane.

They let him in and he goes straight to the fireplace. There is no sign of Mary. Then, somewhere in the flue, Sparrow hears a terrible wailing. With the help of the surprised inhabitants, he douses the flames with water until the chimney is cool enough for him to fly up. Inside, it is dark and there are difficult bends. At one stage he nearly breaks a wing by fluttering into a vent shaft. Luckily he is guided in the right direction by Mary's cries and, after considerable difficulty, is able to find her. She has fallen onto a protruding ledge halfway up the flue and is unable to move. Huge soot-rats, some the length of a cat, surround her and taunt her with jeers and insults. However, when the cowardly soot-rats see Sparrow, they flee, fearing an attack from the sharp beak. Only Head Soot-Rat remains. He wants to know Mary's business in his flue.

You can't just come wandering in like this. Didn't you know this was private property. Who do you think you are . . .

Sparrow tells Head Soot-Rat to shut up. He explains that it was an accident and Mary had no wish to interfere. Head Soot-Rat, realising he has made a fool of himself, apologises and grudgingly asks if we need any help to get Mary down. He calls an assistant who brings rope-ladders and axes. Unfortunately the fire has picked up again and it is now far too hot to descend. Sparrow calls down and asks the inhabitants to throw on water. They are disagreeable and refuse. So Sparrow and Mary piss and soon the flames die. Mary, grunting, growling and now suffering from an almighty hang-over, is carefully lowered down the flue until her feet touch the smouldering coals. The inhabitants, still livid at the intrusion, order us to leave at once.

Sparrow apologises to us for a restless and uncomfortable night and offers to guide us to the all-night public baths where we could wash away some of the soot and grime. We ring the admittance bell but the attendant will not let us in. I'm sorry, there's been an accident. I have had to close the baths till dawn. A few moments later, an ambulance draws up and stretcher men rush in. Apparently, an elderly man had forgotten to turn off his bath water and had fallen asleep. We wait patiently in the transport café across the road until the attendant can admit us. After an hour and a half, he gives a signal and we enter eagerly. It is surprising that the place is so full at such an early hour. Sparrow finds a vacant private bath and persuades Mary and myself to wash together. It will save water charges. In the big pool, I can make out many male swimmers. They are all nude, flagrantly disobeying the 'costumes must be worn' sign. Then, after watching for a few moments, I realise why. They are behaving in a grossly indecent fashion. Every penis is up and stiff. Several of the men appear to be well over 80. In one corner of the bath, the deepest part, buggery is in progress. This is too much and I shout at them to stop it. But a worse spectacle is in store for me. In the far end of the bath, indescribable bestiality is evident. Mackerel, trout and herrings are being abused and cruelly treated. I cannot bear this any longer and run to the attendant's office. He is sympathetic and returns with me to the bath. He raises a hand megaphone to his lips. You are disgracing yourselves in front of members of the public in a foul and unforgivable manner. I want each of you to leave the pool and go at once to your cubicles. And don't let this ever happen again. Thank you. But they do not take any notice and appear to behave in an even more revolting fashion. The attendant shrugs his shoulders and goes to the flow-out valve. He gives it three turns and I watch with interest as the pool level drops. In two minutes, 38,000 gallons have drained away and the men stand around on the bottom of the pool. For a moment I think they are going to give up and return to their cubicles. But they are determined not to give in, and one of them goes to fetch mattresses from the stores. These are spread out on the bottom of the pool and the revolting conduct begins again.

I glance at the attendant. He is determined not to be made a fool of, and I watch apprehensively as he switches the water temperature from 64°F to 120°F. After giving the supply tanks 10 minutes to heat up, he turns the inflow valve. Immediately, a fountain of boiling water rises from the sluice in the pool wall. I witness an appalling and memorable scene. The men rush for the exit steps – but the water is entering at 200 gallons a second and they don't stand a chance.

Several of the more energetic ones actually reach the steps and begin to climb, but are flung off and fall back into the boiling water. They howl, scream and beg for mercy. Only one man escapes. He is hideously burnt and grovels on the duck-boards. A blister runs the whole length of his back, and his face is torn and running with puss. I return him to the pool. Much kinder really.

Sparrow agrees to accompany us to the outskirts of the town. He will make certain we are on the London Road. When the time comes for him to leave, I ask if he would like to remain and return with us to London. Sadly, he shakes his head and, with a last farewell, flutters away. We watch until he is just a little dot in the sky.

24

I STOP AT THE FIRST PHONE BOX WE COME TO AND MAKE A reverse-charge call to the abortionist in London Sparrow recommended. His nurse answers and takes our particulars. She feels sure that Dr. Attel will be able to help and asks us to go straight to his surgery as soon as we arrive in London. I leave the call-box and am annoyed to find that Mary has disappeared. She was there a moment ago; I saw her through the panes. The nearest building is a large pub called the Three Sailors and I enter, thinking she might have wandered in accidentally. I am worried and distressed to see her up against the bar, holding a double large whisky in her hands. She is already tight and as I approach she snarls and tells me to leave. I reason with her. You can't go on like this. You're 5 months pregnant and drinking this amount will do you no good at all. Dr. Attel in London is willing to help you but we must hurry.

Mary tells me to fuck off and she orders herself another double large whisky. The barmaid, realizing Mary has had enough, looks at me for confirmation. I shake my head and tell her to stop serving. There is a frightful scene and Mary jumps onto the bar. She stamps her paws and howls with rage. The landlord, hearing the noise, runs from his office and orders his labrador to kick her out. There's a little dachshund in the saloon bar who's had one too many. Get her out, would you please. Labrador jumps onto the bar with one leap and takes Mary firmly by the scruff of her neck and carries her out. Mary kicks, snaps and demands another drink. I thank the labrador and apologise.

When we are safely away from the pub, I give Mary a firm ticking off. She becomes pathetic and lies down on the pavement. A crowd gathers and asks what the matter is. I ask them to go away; it is nothing serious. Then Mary is horribly sick. I try to get her to her feet but each time she stumbles and falls again. Too pissed-up, I'm afraid. Her eyes are terribly bloodshot and she asks constantly for water. Alcoholic dehydration is obviously setting in. Suddenly I see a small bird soaring down to us. It is Sparrow. He carries a small suitcase and asks if he might change his mind and travel with us to London. There is nothing more for me here. I'd much rather come and live with you in London. Please, let me join you.

Sparrow rests on my shoulder, Mary lies in my arms and the miles pass quickly. However, there are awkward moments each time we pass a pub or off-licence. Mary begs to be allowed to go in and get a drop of something. But I am firm and, with Sparrow's backing, persuade her to keep off it.

Thankfully, an incident distracts her at Horford Main Road. A hospital is on fire. It is a frightful scene and already all floors are flaming. Three streets away, the fire-station is in pandemonium. The outer doors are stuck and the tenders cannot leave. For 20 minutes they struggle frantically but the doors are warped by recent rainfall and it is no use. The Head Fireman faces a difficult decision. Should he drive his tenders through the doors and do £2,000 worth of damage to the oak fixtures? Or should he ignore the emergency and let 500 patients burn to death? Sadly, he chooses the latter and tells his men to return to their recreation room. As he steals into his office to watch television, he can hear terrible groaning just a few streets away.

Matron, sisters and staff nurses do all they can; but it is of little use. Patients who are fit enough throw themselves from windows into catch-nets erected by neighbours. The landlord of

the Bull and Hutch opposite does great work and organises a water-chain. They have no buckets and instead resort to pint beer mugs. It is well meant but useless and the Matron tells them to give up. Sparrow works feverishly and saves many lives on the upper floors. He guides the sick and the crippled to fire-ladders and offers comfort, compassion and encouragement. Twice he nearly loses his own life by fluttering into scorching flames.

In the theatre, a major operation is in progress. Surgeon, anaesthetist and nurses are trapped by hermetically-sealed doors and die in agony. In the kitchen, the cooks are so used to the heat of their own ovens that they do not at first detect the extra heat and work on. When they realise, all rush to the walk-in refrigerator for temporary protection. It is a foolish step, for in moments they are surrounded by flames and watch helplessly as the ice-blocks melt around them. The Chef de Cuisine, unable to face a slow death by burning, pulls out his vegetable knife and slits his wrists. Mary, restored by the excitement, does sterling work, risking her own life several times.

Finally, when we feel there is nothing more that can be done, we leave and set off again to London. Unfortunately, after walking for half an hour, Mary leaves the pavement and runs into a public house. I yell at her to come back and Sparrow flaps his wings with rage. We wait for 20 minutes and then, losing patience, I suggest that Sparrow should go in and get her.

Mary is up at the bar. Her paws are shaking and her face is flushed. She has already drunk two large whiskies. Sparrow orders her to stop it at once. Mary refuses and orders the same again. Sparrow, determined to halt this physical deterioration, flies up onto her glass and perches on the rim. Mary is astonished and asks what he's up to. Immediately, Sparrow turns his backside into the glass and goes to the lavatory. Soon the glass fills with dark, saffron-coloured slime and Mary is angry and perplexed.

She hurls the glass at Sparrow and stumps out. Stupidly she walks right in front of a dart board and is hit in the bottom by a dart.

Mary is now in an extremely difficult mood and refuses to walk any further. Instead, she crosses the main road and gazes into the window of a butcher's shop. The business does not appear to be in very good state, and sirloins, best-ends and offals are rotting in the hot sun. There does not seem to be any organisation. Recently-slaughtered beasts are stacked on the pavement, awaiting dissection. And inside the shop, the butcher is behaving oddly with some chicken carcasses. He was unable to sell them and they have gone bad over the weekend. At his feet there is a large basket of feathers and he is trying to stick them back onto the carcasses with glue. They smell horribly and he uses liberal amounts of aerosol disinfectant. Tomorrow he will try to sell these carcasses to other dealers, pretending that they were alive-on-the-farm that morning.

There is no till; instead he uses a hollowed-out leg of mutton that he was unable to sell. And worst of all he has no idea of sanitary hygiene. He pisses on the counter whenever he feels the urge. It is disgraceful that this sort of thing should be allowed to go on nowadays and I drag Mary away, lest she touch some meat which must surely be contaminated.

She is still in a foul temper and is determined to make difficulties. She goes into a bread shop and steals 2 eclairs and a Maid of Honour. The assistant notices and orders her to replace them. Naughtily, Mary refuses and runs out of the shop. The assistant gives chase, catches her and drags her back to his shop. He is terribly angry and begins to dial 999, but just as he is on the third 9, Mary slips out of his arms and races into the bakery to find a hiding place. She dives into the rising dough and buries herself, praying that the baker will not notice the indentations. But the baker has no difficulty in discovering her and she is pulled out by the tail. Unfortunately, Mary, frightened by the situation, had been to the lavatory in the dough and tell-tale patches were at once noticed by the baker. It was lucky for Mary that the baker was a pervert: he said he would forget the whole thing if he could interfere with her. Mary agreed willingly to the bargain and walked out of the shop 10 minutes later looking stiff, dishevelled and bloated.

Sparrow is fed up with Mary's conduct. If you're going to go on behaving like this then I'll leave now and return home. Keep off drink, do what we say and then everything will be alright. Mary hangs her head and apologises. She says she has been upset over her pregnancy. Until the termination, she pleads with us to be lenient. So she is forgiven and, in return, offers to carry Sparrow on her back. Sparrow, whose wings are weak and feeble, accepts immediately and thanks Mary warmly for such a generous gesture.

At a big road junction, we see a transport café and Sparrow says he has a good idea. He enters, disappears for five minutes and returns with a Mr. Itte, who is willing to give us all a lift to London in his truck. He asks if we would mind travelling with the load, as there is not much room in his cab. He opens the back doors, all jump in and 10 minutes later we are racing up the A23 at 60 miles an hour. The truck contains 4,000 eggs which are en route to a supermarket in Middlesex; so we sit carefully and I warn Mary not to steal any.

After travelling for an hour, the driver suddenly brakes and the truck stops. I look out of the ventilation window and realize we have been picketed by angry hens. They have erected barricades across the road and it is impossible to continue. I step into the cab through the dividing door and find the driver is in hysterics. At least 5,000 hens are striding about on the road in front of us and many others are perching on the windscreen and bonnet. A Senior Hen comes forward and asks us to explain our load. What are you doing with those eggs? How dare you take them away. Unless they are returned immediately, you will not be able to continue. The driver loses his temper, grabs the Senior Hen and wrings its neck in front of the 5,000. It was a stupid thing to do. There is pandemonium. The hens are now pressing against the windscreen and thousands of beaks tap angrily. In the back of the truck I hear Sparrow and Mary crying for help. A new band of hens has arrived, and they are trying to force their way in through the rear doors. I slash at them with a broom-handle, execute several and frighten the others away. At the front of the truck, things are getting desperate. They have tapped a small hole in the windscreen and already claws and feathered legs are trying to enter.

Fortunately, we are all saved from almost certain death by the discovery of a large can of petrol under the front seat. I open it, light a match and climb rapidly out of the skylight onto the roof of the truck. The astonished hens do not realize what is happening as I spray them with petrol. I drop the match and it is all over. A dreadful screaming, and feathers, claws, eggs and sinews explode in all directions. There is a strong smell of burnt feathers. The few that escape instant death are so badly burnt that they die within minutes. Others, unable to face such an overwhelming defeat, take their own lives.

At the next town, we stop and report the matter to the police. They do not believe us and think we are taking the piss out of them.

The rest of the journey passes without incident and we arrive in London, tired and weary, in the middle of the evening rush-hour. The truck driver asks if we would like to contribute to petrol: we refuse and he drives off cursing us.

25

Sparrow, being a total stranger to London, is alarmed by the high buildings, noise of traffic and rushing people. Also, the other birds scare him. As we queue at a call-box to ring Dr. Attel, a pigeon descends and invites Sparrow back to his nest in Chapel Street. Before I have a chance to prevent him, he clambers onto Pigeon's back and they are off. After a few moments Sparrow realises that Pigeon is a homosexual. He wears women's make-up and is heavily scented. Sparrow panics, and pleads with Pigeon: he says he has never been with a man and does not want to begin now. Pigeon chuckles and says he will have a lot of fun. The nest is furnished in effeminate fabrics and there are bronze phalluses on all table-tops. When Sparrow sees Pigeon's stiff penis, he jumps with fright and flutters to the nearest window. Pigeon lurches at him but is too late.

Poor Sparrow, he is hopelessly lost in a strange city and circles aimlessly for over an hour. Luckily, a friendly chaffinch realises he is in difficulties and guides him to the phone box where we are anxiously waiting. To prevent further trouble, I place him in my overcoat pocket where he will be away from all temptations.

We take a taxi to Dr. Attel's surgery. At each traffic light Mary tries to jump out and run to a pub for a drink. Each time I drag her back and when we finally arrive she is in a foul temper.

Dr. Attel is horrified when he sees Mary. If the abortion is to stand any chance, he must operate tonight. He runs to his office and makes desperate telephone calls to try to gather a surgical team. When they hear it is for a termination, many refuse instantly. Dr. Attel is in despair and cannot even get a nurse, let alone an anaesthetist.

Timidly, I offer my assistance and give details of my medical experience. I promise to handle sterilization and pass instruments. Dr. Attel accepts my offer and asks me to be ready in ten minutes. He goes into another room and, beyond closed doors, I hear him erecting a trestle table.

After preparing himself, he returns and beckons us in. He is not wearing a surgeon's gown or skull-cap. Instead, he wears a very dirty mackintosh and an old trilby. I am offended and ask him to take them off. If you can't make more effort then I suggest we call the whole thing off. Dr. Attel apologises and leaves the room. He returns with nothing on and this makes me even angrier. You're behaving like a baby. I suggest we abandon the operation. Dr. Attel apologises again and pleads to be allowed to continue.

Mary is at last unconscious. She is stretched out on the trestle table and for the first time I realise that she is in terrible condition. Bald patches over her chest and thighs. Teeth mostly fallen out and paws swollen. Just as the operation is about to start, the trestle table collapses and Mary is flung to the floor. She rolls over several times and, because of the shock, regains consciousness. I give her a double dose of Ginshine and the eyes close again. I pass Dr. Attel appropriate scalpels, expecting him to start at once. His hand starts to shake and he feels Mary all over. He does not seem to be too sure of himself and seems afraid to touch her. Suddenly he returns the scalpel and begins to cry. Between sobs, he says he cannot undertake the operation. Then he runs from the room and I hear the front door slamming. I go straight to the window and watch horrified as he walks, completely naked, into the path of an oncoming bus. The driver brakes but hasn't a hope and Dr. Attel is completely destroyed. The conductor, not realising what has happened, rings the bell impatiently. The driver is too shocked to move and vomits uncontrollably.

I pick up Mary's unconscious body, call Sparrow and run from the surgery. We have nowhere to go and wander aimlessly for several hours. As Mary slowly regains consciousness she struggles in my arms and pleads for alcohol. After struggling with her for several hours, I give in and watch helplessly from a nearby bench as Mary runs into the Fox and Vixen. At half past six, the saloon bar door is flung open and Mary is hurled into the road. She had got frightfully drunk, been abusive and pissed on the floor in front of women and young girls. She is in a dreadful state and is clutching half a bottle of sweet sherry bought from off-sales. Passers-by stop to stare as she staggers about the pavement, pissing, vomiting and shouting fuck off to anyone she finds fault with. I am embarrassed and, before she disgraces herself further, I take off my jacket and throw it over her. Beneath the Harris Tweed, I hear grunts, gurps and her sherry bottle shattering. I take her in my arms and, with Sparrow still perching on my shoulder, run rapidly away from the scene. However, a police officer has been watching the incident from the other side of the road. He catches up and taps my shoulder. Your dog is under arrest. Are you the lawful owner? You must accompany me to my police station. What's that sparrow doing on your shoulder? I don't like its face. I've a good mind to wring its bloody neck.

On the way to the police station, we are delayed by an incident at a roundabout. A motorist has gone berserk and is driving his blue saloon round and round. Onlookers say this is his 300th time round. There is no law against doing this, but, for the sake of his own safety, the police have decided to intercept. This is more difficult than they think, and the officers, unable to stop him, call their chief inspector for advice and guidance. He says there is nothing to do but wait till his petrol runs out. However, he suggested that onlookers should be kept at least 200 yards back, and that fire and ambulance crews should be on call in case of emergency. Unfortunately, there was no time to carry out these precautions. On the motorist's 323rd revolution, he was seen to pull out a pistol and shoot himself. He died instantly and his car, out of control, skidded into the crowd, taking four lives and maiming three. At the mortuary, they discovered that the motorist had escaped from Brooker Hall earlier today.

We wait in the charge room while the officer takes particulars. You will attend Court Number 2 at 10.30 tomorrow morning. In the meantime, as all our cells are in use, I shall have to lock you in the lavatory overnight. Your sparrow cannot remain with you. He must be released.

It is cramped in the lavatory. Hours pass slowly and Mary begs for alcohol. I sit on the seat with M on my lap. Sparrow, determined not to leave us, perches on the window sill outside. I see him beyond the frosted glass. At ten past eleven, Mary becomes desperate and shrieks for drink. Thoughtful Sparrow flies to a nearby hotel, steals a lamp-wick and returns. The methylated spirits give Mary some satisfaction and she chews till the wick is shredded. Throughout the night, officers try the door. It is the only lavatory in the building and they are forced to defecate/piss in a temporary tin placed in the charge room. It is not a very satisfactory arrangement and the tin is gradually collapsing under the weight of stout constables. At eight minutes past four, there is an angry scream. The tin has gone over and Sgt. Webe has to wait till breakfast time to change his uniform.

The gaoler knocks on the door at 10. Mary is badly hung-over. I have to steady her and, at the suggestion of the gaoler, take a sick-bowl into court. The magistrate is kind and thoughtful. He deals with our case quickly, giving Mary an absolute discharge providing she agrees to attend Colter Hill Maternity Home and Alcoholic Centre. Mary bursts into tears. She breaks away from the gaoler and runs to the magistrate's dais. Court officials wave their hands at her. Stop it. Get back to the dock. You've no business to behave like this. But the magistrate raises his hand, ordering the officials to be silent. The court is hushed. Mary is on the magistrate's lap and all that can be heard is her sobs. He is stroking her: Everything will be alright, my dear. This is the best thing for you. Magistrate has a dachshund of his own at home. He is almost in tears and so upset that he is unable to take the rest of the cases. He goes home in a taxi and the relief magistrate is summoned by telegram. However, he refuses to make the journey and the court is closed for the day. Major offenders are returned to their cells. Minor offenders (drunks, exposures, petty thefts) are set free.

A telephone call is put through to the superintendent at Colter Hill. Mary will be arriving on the one-thirty train. A car will meet her. The gaoler and a police officer accompany us to the station. We must meet Mary's fare ourselves, so I ask Sparrow to distract the newsagent's attention and lift some money from the till with his beak. The police officer notices but, realizing the circumstances, ignores the offence. Unfortunately, just as Sparrow has gripped on to a five-pound note, the till drawer is shut and Sparrow is trapped inside. Anxiously, we wait for another sale and the till to open. He loses several feathers but otherwise is unhurt.

The train is delayed and the gaoler buys cups of tea at the canteen. Mary will not sip and clutches me. It is pathetic. She urges me not to leave her like this. The train pulls in and she begins to weep again. The gaoler, normally brutal, is visibly upset and takes a napkin to wipe his eyes. Mary, thinking this a good moment to escape, slips her collar and runs. Soon she is lost in the crowds. The angry gaoler organises a search and all station personnel are summoned. Meanwhile the train is not allowed to leave. After half an hour I hear the gaoler cry out. He has found Mary hiding in a waste-paper basket (her tail stuck out). The gaoler has now no patience and marches her onto the platform, kicking her whenever she lingers or delays. All down the train, passengers lean from their windows and boo: they are furious at the delay. A compartment door is opened but, as Mary steps in, she trips and falls between platform and coach. The gaoler goes down on his knees and curses. She has fallen 9 feet and is straddled across a line. I think she is unconscious. The station master brings a rope-ladder and I volunteer to descend. I place wet flannels on her head, and in a few moments she comes round. She has lost her memory. She wants to know where she is.

Now the impatient engine-driver is beside us: I must take my train away now. I cannot delay further. Put her on, or travel later. There is no alternative. I wrap Mary in my pullover and place her in a compartment. But the occupants do not want her and ask for her to be removed. I try next door. Three businessmen tell me to clear out. Finally I am forced to leave her on the corridor floor. As the train begins to move, she staggers to her feet and I see the old grey face pressed against the glass. She tries to say something, but her voice cannot be heard. Sparrow's tears are running down my sleeve and we wait till the last carriage disappears.

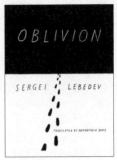

OBLIVION BY SERGEI LEBEDEV

In one of the first 21st century Russian novels to probe the legacy of the Soviet prison camp system, a young man travels to the vast wastelands of the Far North to uncover the truth about a shadowy neighbor who saved his life, and whom he knows only as Grandfather II. Emerging from today's Russia, where the ills of the past are being forcefully erased from public memory, this masterful novel represents an epic literary attempt to rescue history from the brink of oblivion.

THE 6:41 TO PARIS BY JEAN-PHILIPPE BLONDEL

Cécile, a stylish 47-year-old, has spent the weekend visiting her parents outside Paris. By Monday morning, she's exhausted. These trips back home are stressful and she settles into a train compartment with an empty seat beside her. But it's soon occupied by a man she recognizes as Philippe Leduc, with whom she had a passionate affair that ended in her brutal humiliation 30 years ago. In the fraught hour and a half that ensues, Cécile and Philippe hurtle towards the French capital in a psychological thriller about the pain and promise of past romance.

THE LAST WEYNFELDT BY MARTIN SUTER

Adrian Weynfeldt is an art expert in an international auction house, a bachelor in his mid-fifties living in a grand Zurich apartment filled with costly paintings and antiques. Always correct and well-mannered, he's given up on love until one night—entirely out of character for him—Weynfeldt decides to take home a ravishing but unaccountable young woman and gets embroiled in an art forgery scheme that threatens his buttoned up existence. This refined page-turner moves behind elegant bourgeois facades into darker recesses of the heart.

ANIMAL INTERNET BY ALEXANDER PSCHERA

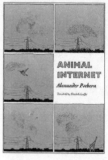

Some 50,000 creatures around the globe—including whales, leopards, flamingoes, bats and snails—are being equipped with digital tracking devices. The data gathered and studied by major scientific institutes about their behavior will warn us about tsunamis, earthquakes and volcanic eruptions, but also radically transform our relationship to the natural world. Contrary to pessimistic fears, author Alexander Pschera sees the Internet as creating a historic opportunity for a new dialogue between man and nature.

GUYS LIKE ME BY DOMINIQUE FABRE

Dominique Fabre, born in Paris and a life-long resident of the city, exposes the shadowy, anonymous lives of many who inhabit the French capital. In this quiet, subdued tale, a middle-aged office worker, divorced and alienated from his only son, meets up with two childhood friends who are similarly adrift. He's looking for a second act to his mournful life, seeking the harbor of love and a true connection with his son. Set in palpably real Paris streets that feel miles away from the City of Light, a stirring novel of regret and absence, yet not without a glimmer of hope.

KILLING AUNTIE BY ANDRZEJ BURSA

A young university student named Jurek, with no particular ambitions or talents, finds himself with nothing to do. After his doting aunt asks the young man to perform a small chore, he decides to kill her for no good reason other than, perhaps, boredom. This short comedic masterpiece combines elements of Dostoevsky, Sartre, Kafka, and Heller, coming together to produce an unforgettable tale of murder and—just maybe—redemption.

I Called Him Necktie by Milena Michiko Flašar

Twenty-year-old Taguchi Hiro has spent the last two years of his life living as a hikikomori—a shut-in who never leaves his room and has no human interaction—in his parents' home in Tokyo. As Hiro tentatively decides to reenter the world, he spends his days observing life from a park bench. Gradually he makes friends with Ohara Tetsu, a salaryman who has lost his job. The two discover in their sadness a common bond. This beautiful novel is moving, unforgettable, and full of surprises.

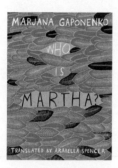

Who is Martha? by Marjana Gaponenko

In this rollicking novel, 96-year-old ornithologist Luka Levadski foregoes treatment for lung cancer and moves from Ukraine to Vienna to make a grand exit in a luxury suite at the Hotel Imperial. He reflects on his past while indulging in Viennese cakes and savoring music in a gilded concert hall. Levadski was born in 1914, the same year that Martha—the last of the now-extinct passenger pigeons—died. Levadski himself has an acute sense of being the last of a species. This gloriously written tale mixes piquant wit with lofty musings about life, friendship, aging and death.

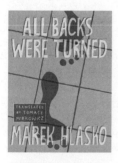

All Backs Were Turned by Marek Hlasko

Two desperate friends—on the edge of the law—travel to the southern Israeli city of Eilat to find work. There, Dov Ben Dov, the handsome native Israeli with a reputation for causing trouble, and Israel, his sidekick, stay with Ben Dov's younger brother, Little Dov, who has enough trouble of his own. Local toughs are encroaching on Little Dov's business, and he enlists his older brother to drive them away. It doesn't help that a beautiful German widow is rooming next door. A story of passion, deception, violence, and betrayal, conveyed in hard-boiled prose reminiscent of Hammett and Chandler.

ALEXANDRIAN SUMMER BY YITZHAK GORMEZANO GOREN

This is the story of two Jewish families living their frenzied last days in the doomed cosmopolitan social whirl of Alexandria just before fleeing Egypt for Israel in 1951. The conventions of the Egyptian upper-middle class are laid bare in this dazzling novel, which exposes sexual hypocrisies and portrays a vanished polyglot world of horse racing, seaside promenades and nightclubs.

COCAINE BY PITIGRILLI

Paris in the 1920s—dizzy and decadent. Where a young man can make a fortune with his wits … unless he is led into temptation. Cocaine's dandified hero Tito Arnaudi invents lurid scandals and gruesome deaths, and sells these stories to the newspapers. But his own life becomes even more outrageous when he acquires three demanding mistresses. Elegant, witty and wicked, Pitigrilli's classic novel was first published in Italian in 1921 and retains its venom even today.

KILLING THE SECOND DOG BY MAREK HLASKO

Two down-and-out Polish con men living in Israel in the 1950s scam an American widow visiting the country. Robert, who masterminds the scheme, and Jacob, who acts it out, are tough, desperate men, exiled from their native land and adrift in the hot, nasty underworld of Tel Aviv. Robert arranges for Jacob to run into the widow who has enough trouble with her young son to keep her occupied all day. What follows is a story of romance, deception, cruelty and shame. Hlasko's writing combines brutal realism with smoky, hard-boiled dialogue, in a bleak world where violence is the norm and love is often only an act.

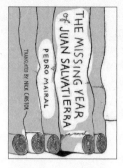

THE MISSING YEAR OF JUAN SALVATIERRA BY PEDRO MAIRAL

At the age of nine, Juan Salvatierra became mute following a horse riding accident. At twenty, he began secretly painting a series of canvases on which he detailed six decades of life in his village on Argentina's frontier with Uruguay. After his death, his sons return to deal with their inheritance: a shed packed with rolls over two miles long. But an essential roll is missing. A search ensues that illuminates links between art and life, with past family secrets casting their shadows on the present.

THE GOOD LIFE ELSEWHERE BY VLADIMIR LORCHENKOV

The very funny—and very sad—story of a group of villagers and their tragicomic efforts to emigrate from Europe's most impoverished nation to Italy for work. An Orthodox priest is deserted by his wife for an art-dealing atheist; a mechanic redesigns his tractor for travel by air and sea; and thousands of villagers take to the road on a modern-day religious crusade to make it to the Italian Promised Land. A country where 25 percent of its population works abroad, remittances make up nearly 40 percent of GDP and alcohol consumption per capita is the world's highest— Moldova surely has its problems. But, as Lorchenkov vividly shows, it's also a country whose residents don't give up easily.

SOME DAY BY SHEMI ZARHIN

On the shores of Israel's Sea of Galilee lies the city of Tiberias, a place bursting with sexuality and longing for love. The air is saturated with smells of cooking and passion. *Some Day* is a gripping family saga, a sensual and emotional feast that plays out over decades. This is an enchanting tale about tragic fates that disrupt families and break our hearts. Zarhin's hypnotic writing renders a painfully delicious vision of individual lives behind Israel's larger national story.

***FANNY VON ARNSTEIN: DAUGHTER OF THE
ENLIGHTENMENT* BY HILDE SPIEL***

In 1776 Fanny von Arnstein, the daughter of
the Jewish master of the royal mint in Berlin,
came to Vienna as an 18-year-old bride. She
married a financier to the Austro-Hungarian
imperial court, and hosted an ever more
splendid salon which attracted luminaries of
the day. Spiel's elegantly written and carefully
researched biography provides a vivid portrait
of a passionate woman who advocated for the rights of Jews, and
illuminates a central era in European cultural and social history.

🏺 New Vessel Press

To purchase these titles and for more information please visit newvesselpress.com.